I0685619

THE THAI WIFE STORY
STAR

THE THAI WIFE SERIES OF NOVELS
BOOK 2

THE THAI WIFE STORY STAR

THE THAI WIFE SERIES OF NOVELS
BOOK 2

BY

RAYMOND GREENLAW

ROXY PUBLISHING, LLC
SAVANNAH, GEORGIA
UNITED STATES OF AMERICA

COPY EDITOR—Marjorie Roxburgh
COVER DESIGN—Robert Greenlaw, Jr.
TEXT DESIGN—Raymond Greenlaw
PHOTOGRAPHER—Raymond Greenlaw
TYPESETTING—Raymond Greenlaw

ROXY PUBLISHING, LLC
Savannah, Georgia 31419
United States of America

http://drraymondgreenlaw.com
First edition, paperback.
Book 2 in *The Thai Wife Series of Novels*.

The Thai Wife Story Star is a work of fiction. All contents in the book are either the product of the author's imagination or are used fictitiously. Any resemblance of the main characters to actual persons is purely coincidental.

ISBN 978-1-947467-21-7 (Paperback)

DEDICATION

Wherever you are, I hope your dreams come true.

PREFACE

THE INSPIRATIONS for these novels are the beautiful and friendly women of Thailand. This is book 2 in the series. The main characters are fictitious, and any resemblance to actual persons is purely coincidental. Parts are historical fiction. No linkage between the events described and the policies of any nation state should be drawn. The author possesses a deep love for Thailand, and no part should be interpreted as otherwise. These novels are storytelling, written for the enjoyment of readers.

The books in *The Thai Wife Series of Novels* use a phonetic-Thai spelling. There are many different ways of writing Thai words in English, and our method is but one of them. For the most part, we don't worry about exact pronunciations and tones. Any foreigner who speaks Thai will recognize the intended Thai words from their phonetic spellings.

I include a Thai-to-English dictionary in an appendix, so you can look up the meaning of any Thai word contained in this book. Anyone interested in learning more about the Thai language can obtain a copy of my book, *Essential Conversational Thai,* co-authored with Saowaluk Rattanaudomsawat.

There are times in the text when several people are speaking or making sounds simultaneously. I indicate this by identifying the character who is speaking followed by an arrow (→). For example,

Tom → "Hello."

Star → "Sa waa dii ka."

signifies that Tom said, 'Hello,' at the exact same time as Star said, 'Sa waa dii ka.' The spatial order of these two lines is not significant. So,

Star → "Sa waa dii ka."

Tom → "Hello."

has an identical meaning.

I've expressed a Thai person speaking imperfect English in an authentic fashion by including the usual grammatical errors, omitted words, and common mispronunciations. Those readers who have traveled in Thailand will recognize these solecisms immediately. I've established a YouTube channel, called *Raymond Greenlaw's Writings*, where you can listen to me reading chapters of the book.

The novels are intended for mature audiences. Although several characters in the story engage in unsafe sex, the author advises against this. I hope you'll enjoy reading this series of novels, as much as I enjoyed writing it. This series was researched and written over a period of 15 years.

Although I've tried to be as careful as possible in my writing, a few grammatical errors and typos may remain. I apologize in advance. I would like to eliminate any errors in future editions of this work. I appreciate any corrections.

Raymond Greenlaw
August 11, 2021

Acknowlegments

A SPECIAL THANKS to Wongduean Boh-thong for her support and encouragement.

A warm thanks to Marjorie Roxburgh for her edits, improvements, and encouragement.

Thanks to my nephew, Robert Greenlaw, Jr., for the cover design and setting up my associated YouTube channel.

Thanks to my mentor, Adrian Plante, for his continued support throughout the last 45+ years.

A sincere thanks to all reviewers and early readers, both farangs and Thais, who provided me with constructive comments. Your suggestions have helped me to improve this novel, and they will help me with the other novels in the series too. I'm indebted to you. Many others have contributed to this project, and a warm thanks goes out to all of them.

CHAPTER 1

I EMPATHIZE WITH the young Issarn girl, Joy, and I hope the Navy SEAL, Tom, will return to Bangkok to see his masseuse soon. Before he departed for Chiang Mai, I felt sure he would propose marriage. I thought he purchased a ring. I hope she's okay, and doesn't do anything foolish.

I don't have much time to work on the novels, as Cam-Tu is arriving for dinner. My Vietnamese lover is bringing vegetarian spring rolls. I'll provide Maker's Mark, which she refers to as Mark Make. Before CT arrives, I want to see how Tom's flight goes.

I navigate to the Star folder. The situation is similar to the Joy folder. There are three-dozen files. I open the file Part1 Star. As a Nobel laureate in literature, I edit on the fly.

The Navy SEAL sat at his gate in Bangkok's Suvarnabhumi International Airport, waiting for the boarding announcement from Thai Airways. The gate area, teeming with farangs and Chinese tourists, offered limited seating to those just arriving.

While ripping the limbs off a stuffed animal, Chinese kids ran around a Samsung monitor in front of the American. They shouted for their parents' attention. The adults never looked up from their mobiles. The kids continued shouting. Only a couple dozen Thais were bound for Chiang Mai.

Tourists examined copies of Lonely Planet's *Thailand*. Monks in orange robes and Birkenstocks relaxed in reserved seats, and played with iPhones. A group of sunburned, long-haired backpackers in tie-dyed T-shirts stretched out on the dusty floor. Staff checked passports and tore boarding passes in half. Broken English translations followed each Thai announcement. Despite the distractions, Tom reflected.

When the American kissed his little Issarn girl good-bye, tears flowed freely from her eyes and ran into his mouth. At her final words of 'Love you ka' and a wave, an unpleasant feeling of separation lodged in his stomach. He missed her. Tom second-guessed himself about not proposing.

I knew he would regret that. I keep reading, and editing.

The poor Thai girl missed her American boyfriend. She felt like a failure. While Tom sat alone at Suvarnabhumi, she cried in a corner of Lucky Massage. They planned to text and talk. Their agreement provided her little solace. She didn't know if she would ever see him again.

Tom took comfort in thinking he would meet Joy again soon. He'd been instructed to travel to

Chiang Mai alone. If he'd had his way, she would have gone too. She wanted to go. Joy didn't understand why she couldn't. He couldn't explain.

Having dodged the kids and backpackers, at the jetway's entrance, Tom handed his boarding pass to a pretty Thai girl. She checked his ID.

"Welcome ka. Go ahead, sir."

"Thanks."

"Ka."

Tom reached the airplane near the front. Only monks were ahead. They fly business class for free on Thai Airways. The Navy SEAL trailed their orange robes.

"Sa waa dii ka. Welcome on board, sir."

"Welcome. Welcome."

"Thanks."

"Welcome ka. This way, sir."

"Okay. I've got it."

"Ka."

The overhead bin provided plenty of space, and Tom stored his bag. Once sitting comfortably in business class, he wiped off with a cool towel.

"Drink, sir?"

"I'll have a double Baileys on the rocks. Here."

The stewardess gripped the towelette in tongs.

"Thank you ka."

Tom looked at the runway and stared in the direction of departing planes. Still lost in thought, he didn't see their shapes. His mind circled in a haze, and he longed for a drink of Joy's magic potion. The

Baileys proved inadequate. His adorable Thai neighbor brought him down for a soft landing.

"Ha-low, MISter, my name Pan."

The lovely Issarn girl extended her delicate hand. He took it. She squeezed affectionately.

"Pan?"

"Ka."

"Good to meet you, Pan. I'm Doc."

"Doc? Li-eh doctor?"

"Yes, short for doctor."

"Oh, you big man ka. Important. Nice to meet you, Doc. You big blue eye ka."

I chuckle at the blue cyclops. Ole boy, Thais won't ever get plurals. I don't bother to correct this error.

"Thanks."

"You stay Chiang Mai?"

"Yes, I'm moving up there for a while."

"Me too. I work there."

"Where are you from, Pan?"

"Excuse me. Here you go, sir." The stewardess turned to Pan, "Khun aow arai ka?"

"Nam bplow ka."

"Ka."

"I order water ka. I Si Saket, in Northeast Thailand. Me Issarn girl. I back Osaka, Yippon. Where you from?"

Although Pan hails from a poor farming family, her boyfriend is a rich, retired Japanese man. He bought her business-class tickets to and from Japan. She visits twice a year. When the weather turns cold, she returns. Pan works at My Tee-Rak Bar. Her generous allowance allows her to maintain a comfortable lifestyle. She even sends money home to family. They rely on her.

"I'm from America. Your English is excellent."

"You America man? America man good ka. I study English school."

Pan withheld that her boyfriend speaks English.

"Yes, I'm American. I like your hair."

"Thank you ka," she blushed.

"Sure. You're very beautiful."

"Korp khun ka."

"Krap."

"You can speak Thai?"

"Poot pahsah Thai dai nid noy krap."

They smiled. Pan's hair framed her round eyes. Two coils dropped down from its beehive-styled top. They resemble asps. Her boyfriend paid for the expensive hairdo, her implants, and surgery to round her almond-shaped eyes.

Tom guessed Pan was twentyish. Her big brown eyes and curvaceous body attract him. Her business-class ticket led Tom to surmise that she has a sugar daddy in Japan.

"Would you li-eh more drink, sir?"

"Yeah, sure. Another double. Same. Baileys. Here you go."

"Ka. Ka."

"Thanks."

When the stewardess turned away, Pan whispered, "She ladyboy ka. Her man."

"What? Noooo way."

"Ka, she ladyboy."

"You're kidding me? I never would have known. Never in a million years. Thanks."

"Ka. She ladyboy."

"You absolutely sure?"

"Ka."

While revealing the ladyboy's secret, Pan's proximity and breath on Tom's ear, as well as her saying the libertine word 'ladyboy,' aroused him. He hasn't come to terms with his feelings toward ladyboys. In the military, he learned the don't ask, don't tell rule, but many of those who are attracted to the same sex suffer from guilty feelings.

A feeling of shame from being captivated by the ladyboy wreaked havoc on Tom's emotions. As a hard man, one with advanced training in situational awareness, the ease with which he'd been duped troubled him. It was more than that though, much more. He adjusted himself in his seat.

Pan leaned toward Tom. She placed her hand on his arm. Her lips neared his ear again.

"Ladyboy man who dress and act li-eh woman. Wery beautiful ka. Male hormone mean firm shape. They tall li-eh model. Thailand good plastic surgeon. Ladyboy breast implant, nose job, hand, and more ka."

"Oh. Really?"

"Ka."

Tom touched his forehead. She touched his Adam's apple.

"A few surgery here. Then, her female voice too."

She pointed at his crotch.

"A few surgery there. Now woman stuff. Those with big organ keep it. Me sure she wery big."

"Oh, my. Really?"

"Ka."

Pan blushed. He fought against his smile, but lost. He shook his head. She twirled her fingers through her dangling hair. First, she coiled the hanging serpent, while covering up her long, red nails. Slowly, she released the ophidian, and set the curl and nails free. The two asps stared at him.

"Farang can't tell ladyboy from weal woman."

"Farang means foreigner, right?"

Tom put air quotes around 'foreigner.'

"Ka."

"She fooled me. Ha, ha, ha."

"Her fool all farang easy. Wery hot lady."

"Amazing Thailand."

"Ka. Wery amazin'."

"Hmm."

Pan's smile revealed a perfect set of white and straight teeth. She detected a change in his attitude toward the stewardess. She sensed his discomfort.

Pan knows that some farang men find ladyboys irresistible, while others dislike them intensely. He seemed to be the former.

Their stewardess stands five seven, and with heels, five eleven. Whenever she walked through the cabin, Tom admired her. She's only a few inches shorter than him. Her pretty face rests on a long neck, and the red lipstick increased the size of her mouth. Her feminine demeanor and appearance tricked him completely. He couldn't believe she's a biological male. Tom sipped his creamy Baileys. He thought about Bpee.

I hear Cam-Tu. I want to be with her. I'll hold my Vietnamese lover extra tightly this evening.

CHAPTER 2

AFTER A DELIGHTFUL dinner, a fun evening with Cam-Tu, and a good night's sleep, in the morning, I find myself alone. I stare out at the Naval Academy's Chapel. Something tells me to get back to editing. I obey.

Tom busied himself on the flight by reading through materials about Thailand. He learned that the country is called 'The Land of Smiles.' It's world renowned for spicy food, exciting nightlife, friendly people, exotic temples, gorgeous women, and beautiful ladyboys. He found confirmation of these facts with tom yum goong, the Vertigo Bar, Pan, Wat Arun, Joy, and Bpee.

Thailand shares borders with Myanmar, Laos, Cambodia, and Malaysia. Kunming with its 6,000,000 residents is just a 90-minute flight from Chiang Mai. Tom deduced that Chiang Mai's proximity to China is the main reason why Dr. Cody Jones, the NSA director for whom Tom is working for while undercover, wanted him based there.

From Ryan Daniels, Jones's other covert Navy SEAL operative in Thailand, Tom knows his first mission will be to plant a laptop for a cyber-attack on Advanced Persistent Threat One—a group of hackers in the People's Liberation Army known as Unit 61398. ATP1 are based on Datong Street in the Pudong New Area of Shanghai. They're a three-hour flight from Kunming. A direct flight to Shanghai from Chiang Mai only takes four hours. Tom thought this information might come in handy.

While stealing glances at Pan, Tom went on gathering basic intelligence. He enjoys preparing for a mission. He learned Thailand is a constitutional monarchy—the only Southeast Asian country not to fall under colonial rule. Back in the day, it served as a buffer between the British and French empires. Thailand's king, Rama IX, has been on the throne for over 60 years.

Thailand has three seasons: rainy, winter, and summer. He expected Thailand to be hot and humid, except in mountainous regions. Winter is in December and January. Although called winter, daytime temperatures reach 80°F. From February through May, summer is stifling. In the remaining months, monsoon rains cause flooding. The humidity in rainy season makes the country oppressive. The heat index is higher in rainy season than in summer, topping 120°F on many days.

Tom's in-seat monitor showed 81°F on arrival. He equated this December day to one in June in

Virginia Beach. He studied a map in the *Sawasdee* magazine. Many of his green-faced buddies' ships docked in Pattaya or Phuket for R&R. Most sailors came away with an interesting story or two. Soon after reaching port, a typical sailor hooked up with a Thai bargirl.

The girls search for farang husbands, or for someone to pay expenses and party with for a few days. After taking care of himself at sea for several months, while on shore, a sailor happily hands that chore over to a young Thai girl. His ocean going fantasies become reality on land. She earns good money in a short time. The cycle repeats.

The Navy ships come into Phuket from the Andaman Sea, to the west of the mainland. The Similan Islands in the Andaman boast excellent scuba diving. The boats going to Pattaya come from the Gulf of Thailand. The eastern side of the mainland is famous for turquoise waters, tropical islands with white-sandy beaches, and the tourist destinations of Koh Samui and Koh Tao. As a Navy diver, Tom wanted to get to the Similans and Koh Samui.

The Gulf of Thailand runs into the South China Sea—an area of active conflict. Tom knew he would be involved with operations there too.

"You, okay?" the ladyboy air hostess inquired.

This time her voice hinted of a male tone. She masked it well. Tom glanced at the bulge in her uniform. He wondered how Pan knew. As Tom made eye contact, the ladyboy blushed for having caught him staring. When she leaned over, he admired her breasts.

"I'll have one."

"Double?"

"Sure."

"Coming up ka."

"Thanks."

They both smiled. As the ladyboy sauntered away, Tom couldn't believe she's male. If Pan hadn't informed him, he'd be in the dark. The ladyboy's voice gave her away, but only if you already suspected something.

"Sir."

The ladyboy set his drink down. On a coaster, she'd written her name and phone number.

"What name you ka?"

"I'm Doc. Thank you, Wan?"

"Ka. Anytime ka. Call me," the ladyboy winked.

Tom smiled. She smiled, and left. He gave the information a safe home in his pocket. He closed his eyes and leaned in the direction of a sleeping Pan. In his dreams, a busy Bpee and Wan were naked on his bed.

***

When the plane landed, the impact woke them. Pan lifted her head off Tom's shoulder.

"Sorry ka."

"No problem. We must have dozed off."

"Doze it?"

"Fell asleep. We say, 'Dozed off.' "

"Ka."

Pan didn't understand. Tom wiped his lips. They smiled. Pan twirled her hair. He pawed at the coaster, checking it was secure. A series of announcements were followed by English translations. Economy passengers needed to wait for business-class ones to disembark.

When Tom stood up, Pan handed him a note. Inside a heart, she'd written her name and number.

"I would li-eh you call me, Doc."

"Sure."

"It would be fun ka. Go out ka. He, he, he."

"Agreed. I'll call."

"Promise ka?"

"Yes."

Pan tilted her head sideways and smiled. He stared. She knew he would call. He's younger, stronger, and more handsome than her Japanese boyfriend. She wanted to start something. Pan likes muscular men. She prefers Americans. Her advance surprised Tom. He now needed to call Joy, Pan, and Wan. Things in Thailand became complicated fast.

Wan came down the aisle. Tom opened the overhead bin. When he reached up, she brushed up against him. As she held the bin open, he felt her pressing into him. He blushed. He became aroused. She leaned in. They smiled. The monks texted on their iPhones. Pan got her bag.

"Thanks."

"Welcome ka. Call me."

"Okay."

As Tom exited, Wan's fingers played in her mouth. She swallowed. He craned. She planted thoughts in his mind. Pan missed Wan's show.

As Pan and Tom walked off the jetway together, an awaiting stewardess directed international passengers to the right and domestic ones left. In a harsh violation of Thai culture, the beautiful Issarn girl surprised him by planting a kiss on his lips. Pan slipped her meandering tongue into his mouth. He reciprocated. She smiled. He blushed. They said good-bye. They went their separate ways.

Tom watched Pan's swaying hips, until she disappeared. The beehive hairstyle and heels made her taller than him. The kiss gave him chills. He would call her at his earliest convenience. She knew with certainty that the two would meet again.

Tom figured someone was meeting Pan. She hadn't checked luggage. She keeps a second wardrobe in Japan. By the time his luggage arrived, the tall Thai beauty would be long gone.

CHAPTER 3

I FEEL THE MANUSCRIPT is coming along well. I reach for my phone thinking it's Cam-Tu. My Vietnamese lover makes a habit of inquiring what I want for dinner. During the coronavirus lockdown, our relationship thrives. We often eat together. She enhances my life, and I do hers.

"Hello," I say sweetly.

"I calling from Providence Medical Center."

It's not Cam-Tu. I recognize the Asian-accented female voice from the hospital. I'm deeply concerned. It's the same woman who reported my father's death. He died at PMC recently from coronavirus.

"Yes."

"You mother pass away this afternoon. I terrible sorry."

"Oh, my God. Noooo!"

"I sorry, sir. Uh, him doctor here."

"Hello."

"Yes, hello. Is my mother dead?"

"Yes, I'm so sorry … unfortu …"

"How did she pass?"

"Her cough worsened. We tried several medications. Nothing helped. No one has a handle on COVID-19. I'm sorry. We're so terribly, terribly sorry. We did everything we could. I assure you. She went peacefully. If she'd been awake …"

"Oh …"

I pause. Nothing can be done. I love my mother so much. She's gone. Everything is happening too fast.

"Thanks, doctor. Thanks for caring … for caring for her as well … as well, as you could."

"I'm … I'm so sorry … for your loss."

"Sir?"

The Asian receptionist came back on the line.

"Yes."

"You talk mother you every day. I wery sorry you, sir. I meet you mother. She kind woman. Nice lady. Medical center send you her thin'. Send paperwork. Due delay post deliver, you not receive package week. Maybe two. Sir?"

"Thank you … I understand. You've been very kind—first with my Dad and now with Mom. I appreciate it. Every day you report to work, it's dangerous. I respect and value healthcare workers, especially in these times … especially you. I … I would … I would like to send you something. Would you include your contact information in the package?"

"Oh, sir. Please, you no need do that."

"No, I would like to. Please?"

"Okay. That fine, sir. I do that, sir."

"Oh, God. Thank you … thanks."

"Are you okay, sir?"

"No … I mean yes. No … I'll be okay."

"Sir, please take care."

"Okay. You too. Good-bye."

"Good-bye, sir. Sorry."

"Thanks."

The tears drop, as I walk over and stare out the window at the Naval Academy's Chapel.

My heart shrinks, as pieces break off and melt. My mother and I shared so many great times. She was always there. As a child, she made me her priority. I was a demanding and energetic little boy. My mother saved her energy for me. My father understood our closeness.

Whether it was playing a game, quizzing me on vocabulary, baking cookies, driving me to an event, or checking an essay for grammar, my mother always had time. Her encouragement, support, and love made me the man who I am. I need to borrow her extraordinary courage to carry on. I need to face life on my own. My family is gone.

The coronavirus claimed my parents. I wish I could have called Mom one more time. Although she coughed liked crazy, Mom never let on how ill she was. I'm frustrated. We always ended our conversations by stating our love.

As of late, Mom struggled to talk due to her sore throat and fatigue. One call needed to be the last. I didn't anticipate it so soon. Oh, Christ. She never wanted me to worry. Oh, Mom. What will I do? I'm not okay. I'm definitely not okay, at all.

The damn coronavirus kept us apart. I'm troubled. The hospital staff are good, but they aren't family. My parents died alone. Their lives were long and fulfilling, but I never dreamed I wouldn't be with them at the end. Oh, cruel world. I babble and spew expletives.

The pit in my stomach will be there for many months, maybe years. The hole in my heart will be there forever. I'm alone and with no family. I raise a forearm and wipe my eyes. I cry desperately. I look up and stare out at the Naval Academy's Chapel.

I'm lonely. I shouldn't be alone.

***

Cam-Tu arrives. I try to pull myself together. I fail.

"Oh no, what happen? Here. Let me put down thin'."

"CT, the hospital called. My mother passed away ... passed this afternoon."

"Oh, noooo!"

Cam-Tu raises both hands to her mouth.

"Yes, I spoke to a woman and doctor. Mom passed peacefully. I'm such a mess. I've lost them in such a short time. It's not the same thing as a car accident. You know? Fucking coronavirus. No, no, no! Oh, I'm sorry. Oh, God. It's a disease … a disease with no cure."

"Oh, me so sorry you. You, okay?"

"You know … my heart is broken. Yes, I'm okay. No, not really … I'm trying. No, I guess I'm not okay. I'm not … I'm probably not okay. I love my mother so much. First, it's my father. And, now Mom. Both gone … both gone, gone forever.

"I'll never see them again. Never see their smiles. Never go fishing with Dad. Never take a walk. Never hear Mom laugh or sing. Never feel her touch. Never taste her cooking. Never hear her opinions … Dad was funny. Great sense of humor. Never hear his jokes. Never get his opinions.

"Oh, it's just so hard. Both at once. It's good I'm not … not working at the Academy. I wouldn't be a good professor. I'm a mess, CT … I'm a fucking mess. A couple months ago, no one ever heard of … of the coronavirus. Now my folks are … are dead. You need to be careful, CT. I can't believe this. I'm rambling. It's just … this is so … uh, hard. And … uh, unexpected. I thought … I thought my parents would be around for … for … for at least another ten years. I don't know. I don't know shit.

"I mean in … they died young. Have you seen the number of deaths from corona? It's growing. They had four-hundred deaths in Rhode Island, where my parents live … lived … and died. Rhody is the smallest state. Not many people even live there. What? A million. Ten-thousand cases. I want a cure—a vaccine or something. We're so fragile."

"Oh, it hurt. Okay, okay. It hurt. You sad."

I lead Cam-Tu to the window. She's a wonderful listener. We look across Spa Creek. We stand there holding hands. I stare at the Naval Academy's Chapel. Time takes a back seat.

Having my little Vietnamese angel here helps me to remain sane. I nearly lose it. CT is a beautiful and warm-hearted lady. I give her a deep kiss to ease my pain. We move to the bedroom.

Chapter 4

WHEN I COULDN'T concentrate, I lost time. Those days are lost, gone, not just to writing. There's a huge void. My mother's death came as a big shock. I suppose it shouldn't have. The coronavirus is deadly. Being unable to see her prevented me from knowing her condition. She never let on things were getting worse.

Cam-Tu's arrival, right after the dreadful news, was a great blessing. Through the troubling deaths of my parents, she's supporting me wonderfully. They died from something medicine doesn't understand, can't prevent, and can't treat. In the US, we don't know where the virus originated. We have little information. No vaccine is in sight.

Worse is humanity's feeling of helplessness and the unknown. No one knows the end game. The contradictory information in the media only serves to increase distrust of politicians and the government. COVID-19 brings out the best in some, and the worst in others. Throughout the nation, tension is building, and I hope it doesn't lead to something as destructive as racial riots.

Cam-Tu's compassion and companionship has helped me through this difficult period. Without her love and support, I would be in a deep, dark hole. I couldn't have survived the pandemic alone. I'm sure I couldn't.

CT understands my feelings, and speaks the right words, at the right time. She never says too much, but somehow knows the right amount. Her words flow with empathy. It's more than words. Her sensitivity and instincts are remarkable, and I consider myself a lucky man. She's special.

Cam-Tu is encouraging me to get back to writing. She doesn't want me to rush, but senses that starting work again will assist in my healing and recovery. At this unbearable crisis, I'm not sure about the quality that I'll be able to produce. But, based on her advice, I'm giving it a shot.

Other Nobel laureates wrote their best material from prison cells, or when under extreme duress. My work is different. I'm editing an interesting, well-written, and nearly complete narrative. On that fateful day, I discovered these novels on this laptop, which I found here in my rental apartment at the Tecumseh. Thank God, the Naval Academy's Dean granted me a one-year sabbatical from my distinguished professorship in the English Department. I'm in no condition to teach; I'm in no condition to be around others. I don't feel stable. I feel unstable.

In an effort to get back to work on *The Thai Wife Series of Novels*, I locate the Star folder. I open it; I reorient. I feel better already. A writer needs to write. It's in our blood.

Let me bring you up to speed, as I try to bring the writing in *The Thai Wife Story Star* up to the Nobel level. Pan, the lovely Issarn girl on Tom's flight, had planted a wet French kiss on him at Chiang Mai's Airport. She resettled and returned to work at the My Tee-Rak Bar. After clearing a few hurdles, Tom adjusted well to the northern Thai city.

I'm sharing this information with you because I decided that those small obstacles, which Tom overcame, aren't central to the text, and I deleted them. I hold many fond memories from Chiang Mai. They improve my mental state. My Vietnamese savior's assessment proves correct. I continue in Part3Star.

CHAPTER 5

THE NAVY SEAL rented a place on the northern outskirts of Chiang Mai in a district called Chang Phueak. His three-bedroom house in Baan Ketawa more than meets his needs. The rent is reasonable, and the sisters running the establishment are friendly, well organized, and helpful. Off a little soi, the gated community offers peace and quiet, lush gardens with ample shade, and a swimming pool. Tom makes use of their small gym.

To the west of Baan Ketawa sprawls the mountains of Doi Suthep-Pui National Park. To the east snakes 700-Year Old Stadium Road, running along a shallow canal. During the rainy season, the canal accommodates the rainfall draining off the mountains. Whenever it rains heavily for a few days, the canal overflows. Although a few miles from the red-light district, Tom's house meets his other requirements.

At the base of the mountains, Tom discovered an athletic complex along 700-Year Old Stadium

Road. The public facility hosted the 1995 Southeast Asian Games. There he found a shooting range, an Olympic-sized swimming pool, tennis courts, a velodrome, a perimeter jogging track, basketball courts, a synthetic track, a weight room, badminton courts, a locker-room, restrooms, a sporting-goods shop, a café, an office selling annual passes, and a large parking lot. He reaches the stadium easily by running a couple of miles on a dirt path alongside the canal. A walk/jog gets the tired SEAL back home.

When Tom goes the other way, by winding through a muddle of sois, he arrives at Huay Kaew Road. This road, Route 1004, terminates in the northwest of the city at the Chiang Mai Zoo, and in the southeast at the Koo Muang—the 700-year-old moat surrounding the ancient city. Suthep Road borders Chiang Mai University in the south, and Huay Kaew Road borders it in the north. The expansive campus lies just south of the zoo, in the foothills.

Tom was pleased about finding a comfortable place to live and for getting the lay of the land. His exercise routine provides an outlet. The pace is slower than Bangkok. He felt better. The cooler temperatures helped, as did being closer to nature.

***

As Ryan Daniels had instructed, during their planning meeting at the Bamboo Bar in Bangkok, Tom opened an account at SIAM Commercial Bank's Chiang Mai University branch. The all-female staff, dressed in bright-purple uniforms, helped him setup an account. The charming girls filled out his application. The entire staff got involved. After signing a half-dozen forms, they gave him a passbook and an ATM card. They almost forgot to return his passport. Everyone smiled at the handsome American.

Per Ryan's earlier request, Tom texted his account number. When he updated the passbook again, he saw that Ryan had been depositing about 2,000 dollars per day. Combined with his initial deposit, Tom would soon be a Thai millionaire. He nodded, and secured the book in his front pocket.

***

While exploring the meandering sois to campus, Tom spotted an astonishingly beautiful young Thai woman. He already passed a woman shouting the price of noodles, a hairdresser, a beautician doing nails, a woman running a laundromat, a massage parlor with chatty girls, a lady cutting durian, women washing and stacking vegetables, a nurse in white heels, a girl making Thai tea, a woman lighting incense sticks, ladies giving alms, a clerk in a 7-11 uniform, a lady carrying eggs, a mother beating her child, a woman blowing on dying coals, a strong lady moving a gas canister, university students in short skirts and heels riding sidesaddle on motorcycles, a shopper with curlers, a well-dressed woman exiting a BMW, a woman cooking gai yaang, a lady marketing jewelry, a girl peddling squirt guns and plastic toys, a woman blending fruit shakes, girls playing roadside, a woman selling lottery tickets, a gardener taking selfies, a girl dumping dirty water, a lady in tights leaving a yoga studio, a woman making to-order som tam, a seamstress, a woman dipping dumplings into oil, a girl stirring nuts in a smoky fire pit, a lady peeling mangoes, a girl carving soap, a woman scooping ice cream, a farmer carrying bags of her rambutan, a lady butchering a pig, a schoolgirl arranging hair ties, a woman flipping through a book, a girl in a telephone shop, a lady putting curry into a plastic bag, a waitress, a matron carrying an armful of folders, a tipsy gal selling shots, a woman knitting, a girl delivering milk, a proprietor dusting off trinkets, a window shopper admiring gold chains, ladies making crafts, a woman painting, a girl changing a watch battery, a lady snipping flowers, a woman selling fish and puppies, a student at an Internet café, a customer trying on heels, girls brewing coffee, a woman grilling meat engulfed in billowing smoke, a woman putting on makeup, a lady assisting a girl trying on uniforms, a woman selling accessories, a lady organizing a sock display, a girl purchasing lingerie, a lady buying sweets, and a woman selling handbags. None of them required a second glance, but the stunning Thai goddess, with alluring bronze skin and shiny-yellow stilettos, required a triple take.

The enchanted Navy SEAL continued walking, dreaming. Within a minute, Tom realized he'd made an egregious error—an unforgivable mistake. The unforgettable Thai beauty whom he passed was the most breathtaking and captivating woman he'd ever seen—her beauty immeasurable.

Go back. She is unique.

In his wildest fantasies, Tom never imagined anyone approaching this pulchritudinous Thai brunette's exquisite looks. On the day she was born, the angels got together and created his dream girl. Far-better looking than any model, actress, Internet pretty girl, or beauty queen, the dazzling Thai woman in temple-yellow heels possesses no observable flaws. She exceeds his beauty-scale rankings; she is off the charts.

When Tom first saw the remarkable dish, she appeared so fantastic that he nearly blacked out.

"What are you doing?" he asked in self-reproach. "Turn around, you idiot!"

Good idea.

The ravishing Thai beauty compelled Tom to backtrack. He ran a couple blocks. The locals stared and wondered why farangs always seem to be rushing. In his haste, people on the soi seemed to be moving in slow motion. "I need to find her" cycled through his brain. He searched with the determination of a Navy SEAL, but to no avail. Tom looked up at the sky, raised his hands above his shoulders, and shook them. He would have gone to the ends of the earth for the bronze-skinned Thai goddess.

Minutes ago, dumbfounded by the Thai beauty, he was unwilling to accept her disappearance. Although etched in his psyche, the radiant enchantress with long hair, a perfect face, and a to-die-for body simply had vanished. He shook his head. Tom couldn't forgive himself; he simply couldn't. He dripped sweat.

The distraught American mumbled expletives. On the spot, he promised to approach the bronze-skinned Thai goddess, if he ever encountered her again. Tom planned to walk this route daily, until their paths crossed. He would dedicate himself to the Thai language, so he could communicate with the extraordinary Thai girl.

Upset at his slow-reaction time, which he blamed on light headedness, Tom reversed his course again, and walked toward the university. Suffering from profound frustration, he couldn't stop shaking his head. While walking with clenched fists, he gave himself a tongue lashing.

CHAPTER 6

I'M FEELING BETTER. *I'm behind schedule though. I move into Part5Star.*

Tom and Joy texted during his first week in Chiang Mai. They spoke too. Due to her limited English and his simple Thai, their conversations lacked any substance. At good-bye, things always dangled.

Although they missed each other, it was difficult to build their relationship via long distance. Weak language abilities prevented satisfying phone sex. When Tom asked Joy what she was doing, the answer was always the same, sitting at Lucky Massage. It seemed unlucky to her. Tom felt bad. She missed him; he missed her.

Once Tom's work settled down, he hoped Joy could join him. While he was away, her steady income dried up. Her family began to ask hard questions. She didn't have answers. The little Issarn girl felt mounting pressures from financial obligations. She too was involved in a waiting game.

Tom's life involved learning a new city, meeting university folks, sampling restaurants, improving his Thai, exercising at the stadium, exploring massage parlors, shopping at malls, checking out bars, making friends, and more. Every day, something amazed him. At Lucky Massage, Joy ate rice three meals per day, while praying for a miracle to end her life as a sex worker. She was lonely.

As time passed, the frequency of Joy and Tom's texts and calls declined, until finally, he no longer heard from her. When he knew she wouldn't be giving a massage, he phoned, but she never answered or returned his calls. Tom missed receiving her impromptu texts. He worried, and sent a flurry of messages. He pleaded for a reply—a simple reassurance. Tom professed his strong feelings and intent to meet again. She didn't respond. He sought peace of mind.

***

While relaxing on his balcony at Baan Ketawa, Tom's mobile buzzed. It was Joy calling. Deeply relieved to see her number, he gathered himself. He would provide great reassurance. He hadn't been doing a good job. She deserved more. As a young teenager, she needed more.

Tom never used the word 'love.' He missed Joy's youthful and jaunty manner, and her sexual talents. He missed her so much that he decided he would propose. He would tell her that he loved her. If they were married, surely Tom would be allowed to bring her to Chiang Mai. Daniels couldn't prevent her from coming then.

Back in Bangkok's Chinatown, Tom nearly had proposed. He'd missed another opportunity just before departing for Chiang Mai. This time he would follow through. He would marry Joy; he would have a Thai wife. Having sorted out his intentions, he answered.

"Hello, baby. I'm so glad you called. I have something to ask …"

"Doc? Doc, this Bpee ka. Ha-low ka."

"Bpee?"

"Yes, Bpee. From Lucky Massage, the taller girl in shop ka."

"Yes, Bpee. I remember you. I …"

"Ka."

"How did you get Joy's phone?"

"Doc, me sad new you ka."

Bpee's voice sounded feminine. Her voice trembled. Tom felt he was speaking to a woman. He stood up.

"I hope nothing bad happened."

"Me calling 'bout that ka."

"Go ahead, Bpee."

Bpee sensed deep concern.

"Doc, me not know how say you."

"Say it, Bpee."

"Joy dead … her commit suicide. Me sorry you. Wery sorry you ka."

"Oh, noooo! That's impossible. I was just going to … We were so happy. What happened? Oh, Joy! How could you?"

"I don't think me tell you ka."

"Go ahead, Bpee … I … I need … I need to know. Please, go ahead. Bpee, please."

Bpee let him have it.

"When Joy found out her pregnant with child you, her withdrew ka. Her not talk anyone shop and not in rest food."

"She was pregnant?"

"Ka."

"Oh, God."

"Her wery depress ka. You sent she little money ka. Her many expense, and her need money family. They pressure she more money because she farang boyfriend. America man ka. Farang man need take care Thai girlfriend ka. Not just love. Issarn girl need money ka. And, young Thai lady not married, should not pregnant ka."

"I didn't know she was pregnant."

"Ka. Her 'fraid you not came back she and marry she. Her wery worry ka. Me see she crying, alone. Her stay alone ka. Me try help she. Me thin' her want you came get she ka. Her need talk you. She need see you ka. Joy wery confuse. Her only haa sip ka. Fifteen ka."

"Oh, I feel sick. Joy told me she was sixteen."

"No, no ka. Joy haa sip ka. Birthday she two day ago. Me see ID card she. No party she ka. No have cake ka. Her know you, she only see sip. Fourteen ka. The way I found she. Me thin' you not want know. Me sure you not want know ka."

"Oh, that's crazy. She was only fourteen?"

"Ka. See sip ka. Fourteen."

"She lied to me."

"Ka. Maybe you go jail. See sip ka."

"I'm not worried about that, Bpee. Please go on … I need … Bpee, I need to know … know what happened? I feel responsible."

"Ka. Me find rope 'round she neck. The wery bad thing ka, man with her ka. Me hear him. Me go room. Look ka. Me hear noise room. The one where Joy hang herself ka. A fat farang man. Him cut she down and took clothes off ka. He …"

"Oh, my God. Noooo … a necrophiliac?"

"Necro … necro … arai ka?"

"Never mind, Bpee. Go on … please, go on."

"Me saw him top lifeless she. Going into her hard … him fat stomach ka. Bad man. Me pull him off ka. Him hit me. Hit me hard ka. On face too … Him say, 'Coming now. Let me alone, ladyboy.' Me pull him, but fat man finish inside she ka."

"Nooo. Fuck!"

"Him smile me when him did his thin' in she ka. Me feel wery bad poor Joy. Not good spirit she ka. Not good for Thai afterlife ka. The man zip up his little weenie and ran out shop. I no able do anything ka. Me try help she. Him came inside she before me stop he ka. Him dump full load. Smile me ka."

"That makes me sick, Bpee. That damn bastard!"

"I hate see she taken li-eh that ka. Him rape she. She dead body helpless. Him smile me ka. Him shaking she small body. I not know how him get in room ka. Me never see him farang man before ka. Me cover up body she. Police come ka. Take report. I 'fraid they won't find him man ka. And, inside she with that man's come, your baby, Doc."

"Oh shit!"

"Him bad man ka. Joy not know if her depend you. Her depress ka. Pressure family. No party. I guess maybe you need call she more, or bring she Chiang Mai ka. Came here see she. Wery sad ka. Wery sorry. I wery sorry tell you this bad new ka."

"Well, the last few times we talked, Joy seemed depressed. I never thought she would commit suicide. I didn't know she was pregnant."

"No, Joy shame she ka. Her not want you know. Family shame she. Her need you send more money ka. Joy need you return she. Pregnant young Thai girl not wiew good ka. I sorry she. I help ka. Me try help ka."

"That's tragic. Oh, fuck! She meant a lot to me."

"I know ka."

"If you see the bastard who did this, please take his photo. Send it to me."

"Ka."

"Did any of the girls see the fat asshole?"

"No, they all customer ka. Lucky Massage no camera."

Bpee restrained her laughter.

"No, of course ... of course, you don't. Is there anything I can do?"

"Ka. Send me fifty-thousand baht. Me want take care Joy body ka. Send ash family in Surin. Any baht left, I send family ka. Her came wery poor farm family. Farmer Issarn. Me sad ka. Wery, wery sad ka. I li-eh she. Friend ka."

Tom didn't think they were friends. He thought they didn't get along.

"I can transfer you money, Bpee. Please text me the information. I have a bank account."

"Good ka. You electronic transfer me ka. Me send you info. Help she. Me go temple she. Monk say pray she ka. Save sole she. Wery bad karma ka."

"Thanks, Bpee. I'll send you money right away. Let me know if there's anything else I can do?"

Bpee paused.

"Ka. I came see you Chiang Mai? Finish take care Joy first ka."

Joy's suicide shocked the Navy SEAL. He needed time. The image of a fat slob raping his hanged, pregnant girlfriend threw him into a rage. He wanted to meet Bpee and learn more. Tom had questions. Below his balcony, he watched as a dog climbed onto another one in heat. He thought. The ladyboy detected his pause.

"You text or call me anytime. I love meet you Chiang Mai. Me know you wery upset ka. When you ready ka. We meet. I wait you ka. Me no sex with customer ka."

Tom stared at the dogs.

"Thanks, Bpee. Yeah, send me your number. Info I need to help with Joy's arrangements. The things for her family."

"Ka."

"Thank you. Good-bye."

"Ka. Bye-bye ka. Joop, joop."

The ladyboy ended the conversation with two kisses. She desired the handsome, blue-eyed, and rich farang. When the dogs finished, Tom went in and poured himself a glass of Maker's. His hand shook, as he gulped.

I pour a glass of Maker's. That's really rough, ole boy. I thought you were getting married ... settling down with a young Thai wife. Suicide is a horrible tragedy, but at the tender age of 15, the loss hurts even more. With drink in hand, I walk over and stare out the window at the Naval Academy's chapel.

CHAPTER 7

DISTRAUGHT OVER poor little Joy's suicide, Tom decided to call Pan. Out of loyalty, he hadn't phoned yet. He needed to talk to someone. On their flight, they'd gotten along well. The Si Saket girl's friendly nature put Tom at ease, and her solid command of English allowed for easy conversation. Her French kiss, which he hadn't forgotten, spoke volumes.

Tom walked out on the balcony.

"Ha-low."

"Pan?"

"Ka."

"Pan, this is Doc. We met on the …"

Pan felt relieved that he'd called first, because she'd been instructed to make contact with him by that evening.

"Ha-low, Doc. I remember ka. I happy hear you. You okay?"

"Yeah, I'm fine. Sorry I didn't call sooner. I've been busy finding a place to live and adapting to the city. It's much easier to get around than Bangkok."

When a big chicken ran by below, Tom remembered Thanksgiving. Not many people in Thailand celebrate the US holiday, especially outside Bangkok. He'd been busy.

Without my folks, I skipped Thanksgiving this year.

"Ka. Chiang Mai small ka. Bangkok big. Too many farang. He, he, he."

"So far, I like Chiang Mai."

"Where you stay?"

"I live near Canal Road. Not too far from the old stadium. You know it?"

"Mai ka. I stay near Night Bazaar. Downtown ka."

"I want to see you, Pan. Can we get together for a drink?"

"Ka. I li-eh meet you ka."

"You know the Méridien Hotel?"

"Mai ka."

Tom scratched his head.

"It's the big, yellow building, near the Night Bazaar. The corner of Changklan and Loi Kroh Roads."

"I work Loi Kroh. I know ka."

"Let's plan to meet in the lobby bar. It's called something like Latitude."

"Ka."

"Eight?"

"Ka."

"Great, Pan. I look forward to seeing you tonight."

"Ka."

"Good-bye. See you soon."

"Ka. Bye ka."

Tom's guilt mounted over Joy. Rather than sitting around, feeling like a jerk and blaming himself, he decided to go out. It looked like rain, so he grabbed an umbrella. The Navy SEAL hadn't completely lost his mind. While heading to the door, he spotted a kitten in the living room. When he meowed, he noticed the kitten had eight legs.

Although Tom didn't want to kill the majestic spider, knowing it's alive would have prevented him from sleeping. Using a sandal and mop, he cornered the giant arachnid, and terminated it, with a smashing blow from the mop. When he crushed the spider, the handle popped and broke into pieces. He would buy the sisters a new mop. After using the last paper towels, he was ready again.

As Tom walked, he felt better. While hugging the left side on the neighborhood's sois, he wandered. After several near misses with motorcycles, he found a rhythm. The busy roadside sellers and their customers provided distractions. The rain held off.

The Navy SEAL had gone exploring this way several times. When he approached the blue-tarp-covered shanties of a fresh fruit and vegetable market, there stood the glowing, sensational, and gorgeous Thai Aphrodite. He'd stumbled upon the bronze Thai goddess. She appeared to be floating. His heart raced. He cupped it to prevent it from bursting through his chest. His thoughts collided. His palms sweat. He closed his mouth and wiped his lips. Tom stood up straight, and pressed the wrinkles from his shirt. He held in his stomach.

Tom admired the girl's extraordinary beauty. Her skin-tight jeans revealed a perfectly shaped ass that was pushed outward by bright-red stilettos. The ripped and mid-calf designer jeans revealed patches of her bronze skin. He remembered her heavenly skin. He adjusted his shorts.

Mesmerized by her flowing hair, he froze and stared. She turned and caught the handsome statue, admiring her backside. Her gorgeous smile revealed white teeth and silver-dollar-sized, brown eyes. A powerful magnetic field pulled him toward her. To increase her irresistible force, she took a step in his direction.

"Sa waa dii krap."

"Sa waa dii ka."

Tom pointed at his chest.

"I'm Doc."

"Di chan cheu Star ka."

"Star?"

"Ka."

Tom smiled, but felt foolish, because he spoke so little Thai. In the presence of her overwhelming beauty, what he knew, betrayed him. He had to try.

"Khun sooay mahk, mahk krap."

"Korp khun ka. Khun lor mahk."

"Poot pahsah Thai dai nid noy krap."

"Ka."

"Khun poot pahsah angrit dai mai krap?

"Mai ka."

Star blushed. Tom smiled. Although he succeeded in complimenting her, he didn't understand what she'd said. Frustrated by his inability to communicate, he spotted a middle-aged Thai lady whom he thought might be able to speak English. He led his dream Thai girl by the hand. She went along and squeezed warmly.

"Excuse me. Hi, do you speak English?"

"Yes, some."

"I really like this girl. I mean really, really. Can you please tell her?"

Star smiled. Tom grinned.

"Yes."

"I told her my name's Doc, but I'm not sure she understood."

The woman relayed Tom's message. Star blushed.

"Can you please tell her I want to go out with her?"

"Sure. Would you like her phone number?"

"Oh, yes, if that's possible."

After several exchanges, Star's mobile contained Doc's number, and vice versa.

"She wants you to call her."

"I will. I'll call her. Tell her I'll call."

"That's good. She wants to meet."

"Please let her know I'm very serious. I'm an American."

Star raised her eyebrows.

"America?"

"Yes."

"Wery good ka."

Tom beamed. The market woman relayed a message. Star blushed. He learned she is from Buriram. As the gorgeous young Thai girl began to walk away, she lifted her lovely bronze hand, revealing long fingernails matching her shoe color. Her interior fingers bent down, and her thumb and little finger extended. She motioned to call.

With her free hand, the Thai beauty blew the handsome American a kiss. He pretended to catch it, and pressed it to his lips. She smiled. His eyes tracked her runway walk, which embellished her magnificent figure and caused her Rapunzel-length locks to sway seductively. Star disappeared down a serpentine soi. There wasn't anything the overwhelmed American could do about the stain coming through his shorts.

"Her name is Star?"

"Yes. Her name Star in English. Star in Thai Dao. She wants you call her Star."

"She twinkles like a star," Tom said inadvertently. "Thank you so much. You're very kind and helpful."

Although embarrassed, Tom felt pleased. He would get an opportunity to date the most beautiful woman whom he'd ever seen. With a smug grin, he began to walk away.

"You're an American?"

"Yes."

"From which state?"

"I last lived in Maryland."

"I have wery pretty daughter. Would you like to see her photo?"

"Sure."

After the proud mother's act of kindness, Tom felt obligated.

"Here. Here she is."

"Oh, wow. She's really pretty."

"Her name's Ket. She's single."

"Very pretty."

"You're a doctor?"

"Yes," Tom lied without hesitation.

"Well, if things don't work out with Star, let me know. I'm sure Ket would be interested in meeting you. She's a good girl. College degree. Smart."

"Thanks. You're so kind. Thanks again. What's your name?"

"Nickname Cat. See you next time ka."

"See you. Good-bye, Cat."

"Bye ka."

When Tom turned in the direction of Baan Ket-awa, the street vendors returned to their work. Ket weighed the fruit that a customer had handed her earlier. Tom had forgotten about his arrangement with Pan. He momentarily forgot everything. If he was going to make it to Latitude on time, he needed to hurry.

CHAPTER 8

*T*HE AUTHOR MUST *have spent a tremendous amount of time in Thailand. Whenever I read what a Thai says, their diction takes me right to the sois. The girls drop articles and prepositions and helping verbs. They don't use plurals; they don't have subject-verb agreement; they don't use the past tense. They confuse pronouns horribly.*

The writer makes their speech realistic. Thai is more economical than English, and Thai speakers carry over their grammar, creating compact sentences. Phrases such as "You America ka" meaning "You're an American man ka" bring a smile to my face. I don't correct these solecisms.

*In my works that won me the Nobel prize—*The Thai Boy and His Evolving Kingdom, Please Don't Thai Me Down, and The Scorpion Girl from Issarn—*I utilized a similar style. His style is familiar and easy to edit. I enjoy it.*

Because Cam-Tu isn't coming over, I ordered my dinner from The King and I. I hope the young and attractive Thai girl, Bim, will deliver. I haven't seen her since she substituted at Lemon Grass. She made provocative gestures. I may have misread her. If she's working, I'll find out soon enough.

I begin editing the file Part7Star. Before my food arrives, I want to get through more. I'm on a schedule.

Tom rode a noisy tuk-tuk from Baan Ketawa, along Canal Road, down Huay Kaew Road, around the perimeter of the Koo Muang, down Loi Kroh Road, past pubs and many bargirls, to Le Méridien Hotel. With 300 baht in hand, the happy driver sped away. Tom switched off his personal phone. He checked the agency mobile, nothing. Daniels would be contacting him soon.

Tom stood up straight. He adjusted his collar. When he entered the lobby, a fancily attired Pan greeted him. The Si Saket girl looked amazing. He felt good about calling her.

"Hello, Doc."

"Hi, Pan."

Tom noticed Pan said 'hello' rather than 'ha-low.' On the airplane and phone, he remembered her saying 'ha-low.' Perhaps Joy's suicide, or his infatuation with Star, confused him. It wasn't a big deal.

Pan had changed her beehive hairdo into a feathered style. She wore a black-leather miniskirt. Its slits and the stilettos stretched her already long legs. Her crop top left little to the imagination. A diamond glittered in her naval. Matching harpoon tattoos on her arms captivated his attention. Even without the beehive-hair style, Pan was taller than he remembered.

While squeezing the attractive American's hand affectionately, Pan led him to the bar.

"There's someone in the bar waiting for us whom I think you know."

Pan's perfect English and accent surprised Tom. Her speech *had* changed. She even said 'whom.' Most Americans would have incorrectly said 'who.'

"Really? I'm shocked."

Tom scratched his head.

"Yes, sir."

Sir?

"Hello, Doc."

Tom froze. Pan ran her nails seductively over his arm.

"Hi, Wan. I see you know each other. Friends?"

Ladyboy Wan smiled. She spoke English perfectly. She wanted to ask why he hadn't called. Tom wondered what the hell was going on. Wan stood up to greet him. Her spike heels boosted her to eye level.

When the beautiful ladyboy hugged Tom, he remembered her anatomy from their flight. He remembered Pan's comment about Wan's big size. He wondered how Pan knew. While Wan squeezed and rocked for a few seconds, Pan stared jealously. They competed for the handsome American's attention.

"Ka. We work together. We work with you. Check your phone ka. The real one."

"Give me a moment, ladies."

Tom fumbled.

Wan → "Ka."

Pan → "Ka."

Tom stepped away. He checked his messages. Only moments ago, one had arrived from Daniels. It read, "Pan and Wan will fill you in on details of the upcoming op. They're with us, frogman. Enjoy!" Tom returned to the pair of tall Thai lookers.

"This is a real surprise. I'd no idea. You guys, I mean gals. Wow! Sorry, Wan."

Tom shook his head.

"Ka."

"Sorry, we couldn't blow our covers on the flight. We wanted to make sure you arrived in Chiang Mai safely."

"And introduced ourselves," Wan blushed.

The Annapolis grad at last started to comprehend the complexity and breadth of operations in Thailand. The girls fooled him completely. Although embarrassed, there was nothing to do, except go with the flow. Thailand held many surprises for Tom, as did Dr. Jones and Daniels.

"You girls are good."

"He, he, he."

"We've been part of the team for a couple years."

"Yeah, I joined six months after Pan. She recruited me."

Tom wondered about their relationship.

"You're a Navy SEAL, right?"

"Yeah, I'm a frogman. You both did a wonderful job speaking the vernacular. And, your accents. I see you speak English perfectly."

"Korp khun ka. He, he, he."

"Let's get some drinks!"

"Good idea."

"Take that table there. It's quiet and private."

The table was in a blind spot of the security cameras.

"Okay."

They drank blue kamikazes. The first round disappeared quickly, and another arrived. Although they knew his name, everyone agreed it best to call him Doc, as everyone else did in Thailand. When Tom gave himself that title to hide his identity from Joy, he never realized it would stick. He liked the sound of Doctor Adventure. The kamikazes made them happy.

CHAPTER 9

AFTER CHIT-CHAT and sharing backgrounds, Pan shifted the conversation to the upcoming op.

"Ugly Gorilla and his wife are here now. We've been keeping tabs on their movements. They're staying out at the exclusive Four Seasons Resort in Mae Rim. The Chinese government is no doubt paying. They're returning to Shanghai via Kunming on Thai Airways."

"And, let me guess. You'll be going to Kunming? And, you'll be working that flight?"

"Yes, Doc. That's right."

"Great."

"At the airport, when you enter security, you'll be carrying two laptops. Each will contain an official US government label: Private property of the United States government. Those labels will be clearly visible."

"Ugly Gorilla's wife is beautiful, but according to intelligence, she isn't that smart."

"With my help, we'll manage to have her take one of your laptops. They're identical and loaded with command and control software. We'll basically force her to steal one. When the laptops are in their separate trays being scanned, you leave one behind.

"The security screener at the airport, a girl named Mae, is working for us. Here's her number, just in case. We'll make sure Ugly Gorilla's wife follows directly after you. Mae will delay her, as needed. I'll follow her through, and occupy Ugly Gorilla."

"On board, I'll seat Ugly Gorilla's wife, and confirm she has the laptop. When you board, Doc, you'll make a scene about your missing laptop. You'll gripe about how important that machine is. We'll conclude you left it at security. You simply forgot to pick it up."

"Dummy."

"I'll tell you there's not time to retrieve it, but eventually, you'll leave the plane, and miss the flight. As Ugly Gorilla witnesses our fight, he'll realize he's got something special. You'll insult me because I'm a ladyboy. We're assuming Ugly Gorilla will bring the laptop back, and try to crack it.

"There's sophisticated software on it, which can bridge the air gap. As long as he powers it on at headquarters, the software will infect their systems. Once replicated, the software deletes itself, leaving no trace of the original program.

"I don't know what else is planned. But, once that software gets into their machines and networks, it'll be very hard to detect. It'll periodically send information back to our servers."

"Doc, knows more about this software than us."

"The guys at NSA will be able to determine the extent of China's meddling in US affairs."

"They're also meddling in the affairs of Australia and Great Britain."

"We'll catch 'em with their pants down."

"He, he, he. Ka."

"I see. I see exactly where this is going. Brilliant. Absolutely brilliant."

"Ka."

"We're confident it's going to work. In any case, even if things don't go as planned, you aren't to fly to Kunming. We don't want a record of you having been there. Daniels and Dr. Jones don't want you entering China. Wan will continue with her route to Shanghai, making sure everything goes according to plan.

"I'll fly to Kunming. From there, I plan to take the train to Lijiang, and do a few days of sightseeing. That way, my presence on the flight doesn't raise any suspicions to Chinese CIA. I'll return to Kunming, and then Chiang Mai."

"If all goes according to plan, once the mission is complete, we can meet back here. Those details are for later."

"Yeah, first things first."

They reviewed remaining details. Pan and Wan planned to deliver the laptops a day in advance of the operation. Final preparations and backup plans would be covered then. Tom would review the software and make any required updates. On the day of the op, Pan planned to meet Tom at Baan Ketawa.

Having concluded their business, Tom suggested they go to his place for a night cap. The girls happily agreed. After Tom paid the exorbitant bill, they piled into Wan's car. Tom sat in the back; Pan in front.

A small Thai man moved to the middle of Loi Kroh, held up his hand, and blew a whistle. Wan pulled out in her Lexus SUV, and turned at the Night Bazaar. Tourists weaved through the crowded market. Tom kept his mouth shut about Wan's poor driving. He fastened his seat belt. The ladyboy was drunk, beyond safe-driving and legal limits.

When they reached the north side of the Koo Muang, Tom heard a siren and saw blue lights flashing on a fast-approaching motorcycle. Tom's fear came true, as the cop pulled the SUV to the curb. Dr. Jones had warned Tom about laying low and staying out of trouble. Cody had used the phrase, 'avoid the cops.' They were all legally drunk. Tom banged his fist on the seat.

"Oh, fuck me."

The two lookers smiled and nodded.

Pan → "He, he, he."

Wan → "He, he, he."

"Sa waa dii krap, khun Wan."

"Sa waa dii ka, khun Manow. Doc here doesn't speak much Thai."

"Doc, this is Manow. He's working with us."

A second policeman pulled to a screeching halt behind the Lexus.

"This is Uan."

"You really had me going. Hi, Manow. Hi, Uan. Nice to meet you. Glad to be working together."

"Ka pom."

"Krap."

After pleasantries and an exchange of numbers, Wan continued driving. Tom shook his head, amazing Thailand. He learned from Pan that 'manow' is the word for lemon and 'uan,' the word for fat. Uan is fat. In Thailand, fat people aren't bothered by being nicknamed Fat.

Tom now had two more contacts in the city. They could assist him in police matters. He wondered what the Thai dolls would throw at him next.

CHAPTER 10

I WONDER ABOUT *The King and I, as my stomach growls. When the food arrives, I'll take a break. I need to keep to a schedule. I've much to do.*

Tom led Pan and Wan inside. The kamikazes worked. They felt loose. He thought about Maker's. Out of consideration for their hangovers, he made a pitcher of vodka tonics. They became giddy.

The gorgeous ladyboy enthralled Tom. As the party continued, he became more comfortable with her. He mixed more drinks. Wan desired the muscular American, as did her co-worker.

"What happened to the mop?" Pan asked.

"Oh, that. Long story. There was a ..."

"We want to go to the bedroom," Wan interrupted.

Pan jumped up; she paraded her delicious body.

"Done. I'll bring drinks."

"Good ka."

"Need a hand?" Wan joked.

"Wannn," Pan scolded.

"I'm fine. No worries."

"Ka."

The caravan climbed the stairs. Tom miraculously avoided spilling. After emptying another glass, Wan began undressing. Pan followed the ladyboy's lead.

"Keep your shoes on."

Pan → "Okay."

Wan → "Ka pom."

By the time Tom started undressing, the girls were naked. He remembered Pan's tongue from the airport, as he watched them engage in a passionate kiss.

"You have a nice frog tattoo ka. Big muscles."

"You have a great body ka."

"I like your harpoons."

"I have a harpoon too," Wan said, while pointing.

"You're giant. Look at him, Wan."

"I am, darling. I am. I want you inside me first," Wan begged.

The ladyboy kneeled and looked over her shoulder.

"I've never been with a ladyboy."

Tom spoke in a higher tone than usual.

"We're the best lovers. I know how to treat virgins."

"She's right. Ladyboys are the best."

"You're extremely beautiful. I really like looking. Pan come here."

While they kissed, Tom enjoyed watching Wan's busy hand. She loved his hungry eyes. Pan fondled Tom. Her sober fingers detected something unusual.

"You three balls?"

"Yeah, lucky me. I've got more balls than most people. Ha, ha, ha."

"Wan look at this."

"I am. I'm looking. You need three. You're so big."

Wan felt envious. The alcohol snuck up suddenly. Their speech slurred.

"Me never saw one dat big."

"It's wery beautiful. Look at the size and shap ka."

"I wook ka. I wam."

"This isn't the tam to giff … to giff in ta dah dee tales, but it zah rare cond tess hon called poly or kid ism."

"Pole lee?"

"Say what?"

"Pole lee?"

"Poly … poly or kid ism. Dah whole warld wav two undred case wezz, moss lee in an knee mals. I mean an knee mals other dan hugh mans. I'm rath her ewe neek."

"Lucky wus."

"I hope you an knee mal ka."

"I wam. Ha, hah, ha. They wall fun shun nor mal lee. My med dah call ex sams show I wav fifty-per cent more tes tos ter on dan dah wave rage SEAL, tree undred per cent more dan dah wave rage Joe blow. Ha, hah, ha."

"He, he, he."

"Amazin'."

"Yeah, I set a wecord for the high est tes tos ter on level ever mess sured in a hugh man—giant sil-ver wack wave more. Ha. Hah. You should've seen dah face on nurse who per form ed toes test. Ha, hah, ha."

"I bet she per form ed ka."

"He, he, he."

"You wery hot. The extra tes tos what wever rhone explain it. He, he, he."

"My walls prod duce a kra zee amount of sea men. Watch out, Pan. I won't know man had just two balls wuntil I was lev ven. They don't affect me bad wee in any wayyy, other than what's cause by excess tes tos ter on. I wan wery wast ten kay in boots. More gressive ad tit tude. Get wover here. Ha, hah, ha."

"Doc."

The ladyboy reached to touch Tom.

"Weasy, Wan. Wam not com for table … at weast not wet."

"Kow jai ka."

"Wet me get you whack," Pan slurred.

"Ka."

"That's weal good."

Pan kneeled, and Wan entered her from behind. She let out a squeal. After releasing her own spread cheeks, Pan regained balance and looked up. Tom moved in front. He pressed down on the back of Pan's head and thrusted. The bookends enjoyed staring. From the waist up, Wan was feminine. She has a beautiful face and breasts. Pan's face turned blue. Tom pretended her mouth was Wan. She saw immense desire in his passionate blue eyes. Her grip tightened on Pan's thighs.

Pan recognized Wan's rigidity and rabbit-like thrusts. Tom went deep into Pan's constricting throat. Oxygen starved, her body capitulated. Wan and Tom traded groans. Pan's choking stimulated them all, as their libidos ran amok. The trapped girl convulsed and swallowed. The three gyrating inseparables came simultaneously in an impassioned crescendo.

Once freed, Pan wiped her pretty face. When she kissed Tom, he could taste himself. He thought about the gorgeous ladyboy Bpee. Wan watched jealously. If not for his inhibitions, Tom would have traded places with Pan.

Although there was a go-between this time, Tom realized that sooner or later, he would be alone with a Thai ladyboy. When climaxing, he always saw Bpee. He felt her. Wan knew the American would soon lose the battle against his inhibitions. When he did, she wanted to be there. She didn't know about

Bpee. Pan also sensed that the muscular man's reluctance was waning. The thought troubled her.

***

Tom woke up alone. Pills covered the sheet near his head. Although they'd collapsed together, the girls disappeared early. When he went downstairs, he found a rhyming note: "Call Pan and Wan. You're our man!"

Tom shook his aching head. The gaps in his memory bothered him. He thought about Wan. A salty taste remained in his mouth. He worried and wondered. While rubbing his eyes, he checked his phone. There were eight missed calls from Star, and two from Bpee. He couldn't believe Star had called so many times. The calls came in at all hours. He gargled; he splashed cold water on his face; he called his dream girl.

Chapter 11

M<small>Y</small> HUNGER WINS. I phone The King and I to learn my order was misplaced. I'm assured their delivery girl, Bim, will arrive shortly. I'm excited. The delay isn't an issue. This time, luck is on my side.

The bell rings. I buzz in Bim. I forget what I ordered. The ménage à trois alters my mood. I want to see Bim. Depending on her reaction, if she's done for the day, I plan to invite her in. My hunger for food has been replaced by one for Bim. There's her knock.

"Hi there, Bim."

"Hi, MISter," she says with an omniscient smile.

I stare at Bim's dreamy, round, seductive eyes.

"Um, please call me, Doc."

"Okay. Here you food. It came thirty-four doller."

"Thanks. Thanks very much. Would you like … would you want to come inside?"

"Okay. You last delivery."

"Let me just set this down."

"Okay."

"There."

"MISter, you want special?"

Bim attracts me—her lovely Thai smile and small, young body. She's naughty. She squeezes my hand.

"Yes, I do. I want you very much."

Bim removes her coat. My mind starts racing. Taking her into the bedroom isn't smart. Cam-Tu might smell her, or ask why I'm washing my sheets. Bim might move something. I'll need to get rid of a condom.

When the urn containing my Dad's ashes arrived, I put it on the mantle. Cam-Tu noticed it immediately. I need to be careful. I don't want to screw things up. CT's been wonderful. Think. Think fast.

"Bim, let's go to the bathroom. Lots of mirrors."

"You want blowjob?"

"Yes. Bareback. You swallow?"

"One-hundred doller. You okay?"

"Yes. Yes, okay."

I don't think about negotiating. There's an urgency. I want to get this done quickly.

"And, thirty-four doller for King and I. One-hundred, thirty-four doller."

"Yes, that's fine."

"You okay?"

"Yes, yes. Sure."

"Okay."

Once in the bathroom, I close the door. I could have left it open. I look around. No one can see us. I position Bim between the door and toilet, with her back to the mirror. After removing her shirt and bra, she kneels. I place my clothes next to Bim's. I look down at her chest. She touches me.

"You pretty, MISter."

"Thanks."

"You big size. Wery big size."

I smile. Bim starts what I want. I desire her. She's experienced; her technique superb. While one hand rubs near the base, the other assists her mouth. I lean back and sigh. I watch myself in the mirror. I flex my quads. I watch her bobbing head. My phone rings.

"Keep going, Bim. Quietly please. I'm close. I need to answer."

Bim nods, or is that another bob? She smiles. She understands.

"Hi, CT," I say excitedly.

"Hi. Calling say miss you. Miss you very much. And see how thin' coming?"

"Miss you too. Things are coming … ow, coming … along …"

"You sound funny."

"I'm in the bathroom."

"Oh, sorry. You want call back?"

"If you're okay, I'm okay?"

"I'm okay, you're okay?"

"Okay."

"You voice funny."

"Everything's coming … coming along well."

With a devilish gaze, Bim smiles. She's fully engaged. CT has never gone down on me before, but the next time she visits, I'll suggest it. I miss this treatment.

Bim's teeth stimulate me. She rams me into the back of her throat. My legs tremble.

"What you doin' dinner?"

"I'll probably call out for Thai … food. I like hot Thai … food. I'm making dessert now … later."

"I cook home. Spring roll and rice. Tomorrow, I plan come over usual time."

"I can't wait to come … for you to come … over."

Bim slips in a naughty finger and starts drilling me. I think of Bpee. She sucks and squeezes tighter. I may fall. I keep watching, and listening. Her other hand doesn't slow down its vertical motion. Bim delays the stream with a squeeze. On each release, another gush shoots out. I ejaculate several times. She swallows repeatedly. She refuses to stop. My cheeks stretch.

"You okay, Doc?"

I flush the toilet. Bim works me like a near-empty tube of toothpaste. I shudder. She swallows again. I feel faint. While licking her lips, she reaches up and grabs a towel.

"I feel better now, much better. Just wiping."

"Doc?"

"Sorry, CT."

"Okay, you finish you business. I see you tomorrow."

"Great. Looking forward to it. Thanks for calling."

I flush again. Bim covers her mouth.

"Bye, bye."

"Good-bye."

I double check to make sure the call has ended. Bim removes the rest of her clothes.

"Boom-boom? You good man."

Bim bends over the sink and guides me. I'm not thinking. She's very hot.

"Hard. Bim horny girl. Mai mee sex long time. Love me long time."

I do as requested. We're voyeurs via the mirror. Bim is smaller and younger than I thought. I'm excited; I haven't been in Thailand for a long time. She asks for more. I thrust as hard as possible. Her erotic screeches keep me going. While shouting, Bim goes into a fit. We're sweating.

"You wery good. Dee mahk, mahk. Bim finish two time."

As though I've achieved something big, I smile. She came two times. I delivered for her, and she came for me.

"That's good, Bim."

"Corona. Me no sex long time. Feel wery good. Me li-eh. You big size."

"You have a sexy, little Thai body."

I feel dirty, but Bim brought me great pleasure. We shower together. I ask her not to get makeup on the towel. She understands my secret and obliges.

"That girlfriend you?"

"Yes, she's from Vietnam."

"Oh, you li-eh Asia woman?"

"Yes."

"Asia woman good. Bim good girl. Wery good."

"Yes, I felt that."

After getting dressed, Bim needs to go. I give her 134 dollars.

"You some tip for Bim?"

I give her another 40 dollars.

"Thank you. Wery good."

"Thank you, Bim. You're very good. I like you a lot."

"Me too. Bim came back. You call Bim. I free afternoon."

Bim gives me her personal number.

"Thanks. Great, Bim. It would be nice for you to come again. Please keep our little secret."

"Okay."

We say our goodbyes. After her departure, I'm not hungry. I fix myself a drink and walk to the window. I stare at the Naval Academy's Chapel.

CHAPTER 12

THE CHINESE LAWYER, Ying Yue Jiang from Providence, assisted me in settling my parents' affairs. She worked as their personal attorney for years. Through her firm, Ying Yue arranged and managed their wills, insurance policies, and other business affairs. She coordinated and handled numerous aspects of my parents' lives. The firm served as a go between with accountants, tax advisors, contractors, and even landscapers.

Miss Jiang devoted much of her time to handling my parents' account. Although my Dad offered to hire her full time, as an advisor and personal assistant, Ying Yue preferred remaining at the firm. A large pay increase couldn't entice her. My parents trusted her completely. They'd tried to arrange a date with her for me.

My folks told me Ying Yue graduated first in her class at Harvard Law. They said she's a natural and tall beauty. "She's adorable and smart and elegant all rolled into one, and she has a marvelous personality," Mom had said. Ying Yue and I never had the chance to connect. I wish we could have, while my parents were still alive.

When we spoke, Miss Jiang's voice sounded sweet and informed. She expressed her deep condolences. Ying Yue mentioned that my parents had told her about me. They'd said I'm famous for writing about Thailand. After that, she read my books. She loved them. Once the pandemic permits, she suggested we get together. I agreed with her gentle offer.

With Ying Yue's assistance, I set in motion the transfer of my parents' assets and bank accounts to my name. We'd completed a few transfers before my Mom passed. Although 100 official death certificates per parent seemed excessive, I see Ying Yue knows what she's doing. Everyone requires originals.

Now that my Vanguard account contains over 100,000,000 dollars, I receive frequent messages about managing my money. With Miss Jiang's help, I set the ball rolling to consolidate international-bank holdings from European countries into my Dad's Credit Suisse account. Ying Yue will work on renaming the accounts.

Although I never realized it, my Dad had been a brilliant investor. His purchases of Facebook, Amazon, Apple, Netflix, and Google stocks, shortly after the dot-com bust, but before they were called the FAANG stocks, netted him millions. His long-term holdings in Coca Cola, Pepsi, Home Depot, Johnson & Johnson, McDonald's, Nike, and Microsoft all did remarkably well.

Dad sold his oil stocks, Disney, cruise lines, airlines, and others before the big COVID-19 market dip. He plowed a lot of money back into the market six weeks later. I don't know how my father knew about Nvidia Graphics. When they were trading at 14 dollars per share, Dad purchased 50,000 shares. He made 35,000,000 dollars on that investment. Like Warren Buffet, Dad had a crystal ball.

With the undulating markets, I keep millions in bonds. I have 10,000,000 dollars in cash in Vanguard. Ying Yue and I agree to maintain Dad's positions. I'll continue to follow his asset allocation strategy. I've accumulated 15,000,000 dollars from royalties. On Buffet's advice, I keep it invested in an S&P 500 index fund. I possess more money than I'll ever need.

I decided to buy my apartment at the Tecumseh. Through the part-time office staff, I contacted the retired medical doctor from Arizona who owned the unit for years. He heard I'm a writer. The doctor enjoyed my bestseller, *The Scorpion Girl from Issarn.* He'd used the condo to escape Scottsdale's brutally hot summers. Annapolis's humidity finally made him flee to Flagstaff. He dreads the thought of traveling across the country again.

When the doctor stayed in Arizona, the Tecumseh staff handled rentals of his apartment. During one of our conversations, he made a curious comment. He said a previous tenant from ten years back was another famous writer, but he'd departed under unusual circumstances. Because of that, the doctor wasn't at liberty to divulge the author's name. He let slip that the man was from Baltimore. I didn't dig deeper. I changed the subject. We got along well.

Since I paid cash, the transaction was completed faster than most deals. That's a million dollars less that I need to worry about managing. When the pandemic ends, I plan to remodel. I bought the unit furnished, and the doctor left some nice antiques for me. He said to consider whatever I found there to be mine. He hadn't been back for ages. I simply thanked him.

For the time being, I decided to keep my parents' home in Newport. When I return to my childhood home, I don't know how I'll feel. There will be a lot of my parents' things to sort through. That exercise may prove too painful for me to keep the property. Only time will tell.

I love Newport in the summer and fall. While strolling on the Cliff Walk, I enjoy feeling the Narragansett Bay breeze on my face. I like the smell of salt water. The yacht is in dry storage. Ying Yue's office will manage my bills, until I make decisions about things. She and I need to keep in close contact. I told her to retain my other properties for now.

The Dean and I trade emails. He informed me about the cancellation of graduation and all summer programs at the Naval Academy. I provided my input on questions that he'd posed about online English classes. We exchanged ideas about the department. He described the various travel restrictions in the DOD. He sent me condolences for the passing of my parents. His thoughtful words moved me.

When I informed the Dean about my purchase at the Tecumseh, he was happy. He figures the apartment means that I'll be at the Academy for a number of years. In these troubling times, any sense of stability is helpful. I don't know if he suspects Miss Nguyen and me. She probably hasn't told him anything. She's a bright lady. I'm not too concerned either way, as the Dean is a reasonable guy. I'm not employed at the Academy officially, so there can't be any issue. A lot can happen in a year.

I received a large delivery from Eastport Liquors—nine bottles of Maker's Mark, five bottles of Jose Cuervo Especial Blue Agave Tequila, three bottles of Ketel One vodka, three bottles of Grey Goose vodka, nine bottles of Baileys Irish Cream, five bottles of peach schnapps, a case of La Mascota Cabernet Sauvignon, a case of Marilyn Merlot, a case of Leitz Riesling, a case of Bridget Bordeaux, a case of Inniskillin Ice Wine, a case of Chimay

Grande Reserve, a case of Coca Cola, a case of orange juice, a case of tonic water, a case of soda water, two cases of 7up, a box of limes, and a box of lemons.

I picked Eastport's good wines, and the total came to 4,500 dollars. Even with hand trucks, the delivery guys made several runs. I tipped them well. The neighbors worry that in defiance of the mandatory lockdown, I'm going to host a party. They think I'm planning to invite a number of other famous writers.

I received a significant shipment of food from Whole Foods. Because I normally order my meals, the bulk of what I had delivered are snacks and processed-food items. I can't compete with the likes of Ruth's Chris and Lewnes' Steak Houses. When Cam-Tu cooks for me, she brings the meal over. My kitchen receives little use. I have a nice rotation for restaurant meals. In addition to increased deliveries from The King and I, I order from Nano Asian Dinning, Lemon Grass, and Carlson's.

I meet Bim every other day. The lovely little Thai girl brings a day bag containing her toiletries. I asked her to carry a roll of paper towels and a trash bag too. Bim doesn't mind disposing of evidence. I pay her 150 dollars for her excellent services. She's as happy as I am with our arrangement. She's always smiling.

Although I don't fool myself into believing that Bim loves me, she enjoys my company and our satisfying sex. Whenever I enter, she's wet. Bim says I'm big size. She always comes multiple times. We experiment. I enjoy her creativity and Thai know-how.

When Cam-Tu phoned during Bim's and my initial encounter, it was touch and go. CT has called several times since then, while Bim and I were frolicking. Cam-Tu's voice excites me, but I've learned to remain calmer. Knowing I'm inside her rather than Miss Nguyen makes Bim feel special.

Bim is a sex-starved, young Thai girl. She needs attention, as well as money. The feeling of doing something dirty and secretive contributes to our excitement. The next time Cam-Tu calls, while Bim and I are engaged, I'll put CT on speaker. I can trust Bim. Hearing Cam-Tu's voice during intercourse will make Bim wildly excited. The risk will add to my pleasure.

Bim is skillful. Our afternoon-delight sessions make me happy. I feel free with her. She's lonely and worries about the pandemic. She doesn't have the opportunity to return to Thailand. Although bad for her, it's good for me. I plan to take care of her financial needs. I don't know if Cam-Tu suspects anything, but if she does, she doesn't have a problem with it. CT probably accepts my affair with the little Thai girl.

Cam-Tu and I grow closer despite the fact I'm sleeping with Bim. CT and I enjoy our evenings. The pandemic has changed our way of life. Being confined makes physical contact vital. We feel lonely. Sharing time together improves our states of mind. Cam-Tu encourages my writing and wants to know how things are going. I never discuss details, but we talk generalities.

When my parents died, Cam-Tu was there for me. We share a deep bond. When I need comforting, she comforts me. When I need to talk, she listens. And, Cam-Tu speaks, when there's silence. Our relationship is important to me. It's important to her.

Unless something changes drastically, I want to keep things going, as they've been. I'm being selfish, but I justify that by telling myself I'm a meaningful part of the Vietnamese and Thai women's lives. When the pandemic ends, I can't say where things will lead. I hope I'm not viewed as a terrible person. I don't want to hurt anyone. I'm trying to help.

Despite the distractions and uncertainties, I press on with the manuscript.

CHAPTER 13

I'M EDITING IN FILE Part11Star. I'm upset about lovely Joy still. She died so young. Joy's family must be heart broken. When I think of the fat necrophiliac who violated Joy, it makes me sick. I'm glad Bpee is there to assist. I was wrong about ladyboys. They don't deserve their bad reputation.

It's a blessing Tom met Star. I hope he can move on from Joy's tragedy. He came so close to finding a Thai wife. It's a shame she's gone. His involvement with his co-workers is helping to ease his pain. He's doing real work again. I'm happy we have cyber-operations experts defending America. We face many threats. I'm concerned about our future.

When Tom reached Star, she vented about him repeatedly missing her calls. Although he couldn't understand everything she said, the gist was that if she were important to him, he would have accepted her calls. She insinuated that he was with another woman. He'd been with another woman and a lady-boy. His weak Thai language skills meant that he couldn't make up excuses, or apologize. He couldn't defend himself. His infatuation with Star was far too great to tell the truth.

Tom tried to comfort the Thai bombshell, but achieved little success. However, after hearing his sincerity and sweet voice, Star forgave the American. The gorgeous girl knew that she didn't really have grounds for such anger. Having achieved her goal, she backpedaled on her histrionics. She spoke gently.

They agreed to meet at The Boat—a restaurant off Huay Kaew Road, not too far from Chiang Mai University. Tom couldn't believe he'd caught the spectacular-looking Issarn girl. Star would be his dream Thai girl forever. He didn't want to mess things up. In his travels, there never had been, and perhaps there never would be, anyone as beautiful as she.

After only one day, the beautiful Thai girl worried about Tom being with another woman. Star experienced strong feelings of jealousy. Many Thai women would take an interest in the handsome American. He felt delighted that she was attracted to him. In the back of his mind, Tom already hoped that Star would be the right girl and become his Thai wife. She secretly shared similar sentiments.

Tom arrived at The Boat, and waited for the lovely Thai dish. While standing there, he sweat. Star arrived in a tuk-tuk twenty minutes late. He met her curbside. She asked him to pay. It cost 50 baht with tip. As the tuk-tuk driver departed, while craning to enjoy one last glimpse, he nearly crashed. Tom laughed.

The amazing-looking Issarn girl dressed in a denim miniskirt and a yellow tank top. She wore soaring yellow platforms. Yellow complimented her bronze and glistening skin. With the shoes, she matched Tom's height. He admired her gorgeous face and body. He wore a fitted T-shirt and shorts. She admired his shining, blue eyes and toned physique.

"Sa waa dii krap."

"Sa waa dii ka."

Star offered her hand, and Tom led the bronze Thai goddess into the restaurant. The beautiful, self-centered girl didn't apologize for being late.

"Sorry I didn't return your calls sooner. I didn't check my phone."

"Ka."

"Are you okay?"

"Ka."

"Here. Can you order?"

"Ka."

The server brought water. Star ordered several entrees and two ice teas. Patrons stared at the muscular Navy SEAL and his stunning Thai girlfriend. They made a spectacularly attractive couple. Star looked around. She gripped his hand. They exchanged smiles and squeezes. Their chemistry triggered explosive desires. Although she wanted him in bed, she decided not to play that card.

Star forgave Tom for not returning her calls. His boyish charm and tender feelings made it hard for her to remain angry. He seemed sweet. She realized she could manipulate the rich American. Tom's infatuation kept him blind to Star's games.

The language barrier prevented them from exchanging anything more than small talk. Tom understood Star was studying English. She understood he was studying Thai. He realized that Star actually spoke quite a bit of broken English, but her elitist attitude didn't permit her to make mistakes. With an absolutely gorgeous face and body, professionally applied makeup, and a designer wardrobe, the aptly named young Thai girl didn't want to upset her perfect image by uttering a few syllables improperly.

When the bill arrived, Star instinctively handed it to her handsome American date. The prices were fair, and the total came to 150 baht. She asked for 1,000. Tom gave it to her. Star paid. She squeezed his hand. He gazed starry eyed.

The cashier returned with change. As Star dropped the money into her Louis Vuitton handbag, she smiled. Tom was taken aback, but hid it. He didn't ask for the change. Instead, he returned her beautiful smile. She didn't leave a tip.

After the meal, Tom desperately wanted to take his dream Thai girl home. Star lied and told him she wasn't free. She apologized for not being able to break her appointment, phony though it was. In an effort to make him jealous, she didn't divulge her fake obligation either. Although woefully disappointed and curious, he respected her privacy.

On the sidewalk in front of The Boat, Star took the initiative. She surprised Tom and planted a deep kiss on his lips. He knew public displays of affection violated Thai culture. It didn't violate American culture though. Happily, he accepted her tongue, and they shared in a dreamy first kiss. Many Thai voyeurs who stared weren't offended by the blatant cultural violation.

Tom loved Star breaking with convention. She wanted others to see her with the handsome, strong, and rich farang. When their embrace ended, she lowered her leg, and effortlessly flagged down a tuk-tuk. He gave her another 100 baht to cover her fare. As she sat down, her mouth passed the bulge in his pants.

"He, he, he."

Star poked at Tom's crotch and teased him, giggling erotically.

"Bye-bye, Doc, and wittle Doc."

She waved seductively at his erection.

"Happy to see you. Good-bye, Star."

"See you ka."

"I hope so. Kitteung khun. Miss you."

"Joop, joop ka."

"Joop, joop."

Tom smiled. Star knew she owned him. With smoke billowing out its chrome tailpipe, the tuk-tuk roared away. She waved. He reciprocated. They planned to get together the next day. Her teasing manner and unexpected kiss set his hormones ablaze. With body chemicals raging helter-skelter, he needed a happy ending.

From the moment Star arrived at The Boat, Tom could feel himself ready to explode. The Thai girl's perfect, sexy appearance drove him nuts. His testosterone level skyrocketed. Her public display excited him. Now on autopilot, Tom walked briskly down Huay Kaew Road to Darling's Professional Massage. The friendly massage girls there would be able to take care of his urgent need.

CHAPTER 14

WHEN TOM ENTERED the massage parlor at the Phucome Hotel, he encountered four young Thai girls. They stopped playing with their mobiles.

Pretty Thai girl 1 → "You need massage with Lin?"

Pretty Thai girl 2 → "MISter, I li-eh you shape."

Pretty Thai girl 3 → "Farang. Handsome man ka."

Pretty Thai girl 4 → "Ha-low."

"Sa waa dii krap."

"You speak Thai wery well ka."

"Korp khun krap."

"You Thai wife?"

"No."

"Mai sure."

"I need an oil massage."

"Two ladies? He, he, he."

"Um, yeah. Sure. I'll take Lin, and what's your name?"

"Me name Gai."

"Kai? Like egg?"

"No, me name Gai ka."

"Oh, Gai. Like chicken?"

"Chai ka."

"Okay, sorry. The Thai 'g' and 'k' … oh, nothing. Forget it."

"Ka."

Although Tom had selected the most attractive masseuses, the others were decidedly pretty too. Lin took his hand. While admiring her customer's good shape, Gai followed closely behind. She carried a bottle of coconut oil.

"You need three girl, MISter? He, he, he."

"Let's start with two first," Tom said, while glancing back with interest.

"Ka."

After walking through a dim corridor, the threesome arrived at a private room. The furnishings consisted of a homemade massage table, a few wall hooks, and a faux-wood bookcase, containing towels and a CD player. When Lin turned on the music, Tom recognized it from Lucky Massage.

"We no busy today."

"No have customer ka."

"Oh."

"Good luck have you ka. You first customer come today."

"Take off clothes ka."

"Okay."

Tom stripped down. They watched. He handed them his shirt and shorts.

"You big muscle ka."

"Frog tattoo ka?"

"Yes, that's a frog."

"Wittle froggy."

"Lor mahk. Blue eye ka."

"Him big man."

"Here, I take him underwear."

"Here you go. Thanks."

"It wet ka. He, he, he."

Tom went directly onto his back. Star's baiting left him needy. He was tense.

"MISter, you giant sausage."

"Yai mahk, mahk."

"Thanks."

"Him not excite yet ka."

"Me never see size you."

Lin poured coconut oil on Tom's legs, groin, and chest. The masseuses began rubbing. They synchronized their efforts. Gai leaned over Tom's head and ran her ambidextrous hands down his shaven chest. Her breasts pressed into his mouth. Using both hands, she grabbed him near the base and pulled up forcefully, resulting in a click at separation.

"Sanuk mai ka?"

"That's good, Gai."

"Ka."

Lin started at Tom's feet, sliding up to his inner thighs, and timing her arrival to replace Gai's hands. He pointed his toes. Lin raced her squeezing hands up and down, before playing below. Gai watched. Lin felt something strange.

"Him three ball."

"You three ball ka?"

"Chai three ka."

"Ka. Look."

"Wow ka."

"Yeah, I have three balls."

"Lin never see three."

"Me too. Gai not see three ka."

"Him weally three ball. Me no joke ka."

"Take a closer look. Everything's normal. I mean … other than having three. Touch them. I was born like this. It's a rare condition called … oh, don't worry. I'm normal, except with much more volume."

"Wolume ka?"

"You'll see," Tom grinned.

"Wery interesting ka."

"Chorp. Chorp mahk ka."

The masseuses wanted the other girls to see. Otherwise, no one would believe them. They continued working. They marveled. Tom's skin tingled. He whiffed coconut oil. He flexed his quads.

Lin returned to his feet. The masseuses continued coordinating. Their four hands fulfilled one of

Tom's fantasies. The girls tripped nerves everywhere. He closed his eyes. As their hands traveled vertically, he imagined performing on top of Star. She was somehow closer.

"MISter, you good body."

"Me li-eh you ka."

"Good shape."

"Where you from, MISter?"

Tom opened his eyes.

"America. I'm American. The U-S-A."

"America man good ka."

"I li-eh America man."

"You wery big sausage. Lin 'fraid black man."

"I'm white."

"Me 'fraid you too ka."

"What name you, MISter?"

"Doc."

"Doc?"

"Yeah, Doc."

"Oh, you big man ka. You doctor?"

"Yes, I'm a doctor," Tom said plainly.

"Him doctor."

"Smart man ka."

"Me li-eh frog tattoo. You in America ka?"

"Yeah, I got it there."

"MISter, friend want see size you and three ball ka. Her not believe. I get other two girl. We eight-hand massage ka?"

"You okay ka?"

"Eight hands?"

"Ka."

"All right."

Tom decided to double his pleasure. The masseuses were playful and fun. Two more sets of hands couldn't hurt. He smiled, while thinking of a childhood friend who once told him never to look a gift horse in the mouth. He thought of the eight hands massage, as a gift from Thailand. With four masseuses, he anticipated an incredibly happy ending.

CHAPTER 15

THE NAVY SEAL had taken little convincing to add four more hands to his massage. Lin returned with the others. Gai's hands slowed down. She wished Lin had been gone longer. Gai felt excited. Lin had informed the others of Doc's anatomical secret. The masseuses were giggling.

"No customer today. Lin lock door. This Tin, and she name Nan. Him Doc ka."

"Nice to meet you."

"Ka."

"Wow, MISter, big size. Wery big size ka."

"Him three ball. Me say you. Look ka."

"Mai sure."

"MISter, you three ball?"

"Yes, born with three. Trust me, they work fine."

"Nan never see three ball ka."

"Tin never see three ball. Jing-jing ka."

"Take a look girls. Go ahead. Make yourself at home. Touch me. They don't bite."

"Him joke me ka."

"Three ball ka."

"Mai kow jai ka."

"Oil. Here ka."

"More coconut oil."

"MISter, di chan chi bpak ka."

"I'm covered in oil. Use your hands, not your mouth."

"Good idea ka."

"Here, Tin and Nan. Gai, you there."

Tin → "Kow jai ka."

Nan → "Ka."

Gai → "Dee ka."

"Lin, you go on top."

"Ka. Dee mahk ka."

The masseuses surrounded the table in a square formation.

"All eight hand fit. MISter, you wery huge. Wery pretty, MISter. Me li-eh wery much."

"Him need three ball ka. Him size need."

Lin → "See ka."

Gai → "Me say ka."

Nan → "Him three ball ka."

"Kow jai ka."

"Weally, me never see before ka."

The Thai girls smiled, laughed, and jerked up and down. They enjoyed their work; they marveled at his size, shape, and extra. Tom instructed them to synchronize. Their oily hands ascended and descended, as a team.

"One, two. Neung, sorng. Up, down. All the way over. Only last hand not coming off. Back down hard to the bottom, together. Squeeze. Good, girls. Don't worry, you won't hurt me. Squeeze harder."

"Chorp ka."

"Sanuk mahk ka."

"MISter, I wet. Next time boom-boom ka."

"Me too ka."

"Next time. Keep going. Squeeze harder. Not too fast, find a good rhythm … yeah, yeah, like that. That's good. Real good. Work together. Yeah, girls."

Tom watched and smiled. He tensed his muscles. The girls focused.

"Ka."

"MISter, phone you."

"Ka, MISter."

Tom could tell Star was calling. His swimmers wanted air. He wanted to hear the bronze Thai goddess's voice, but he feared she would hear the masseuses. The girls giggled and made sexy noises. He considered asking them to be quiet.

"MISter, mobile you."

"I can't answer it. Keep going. Harder, faster, farther."

"Oh, that good, MISter. Reo mahk, mahk."

"You wery hard."

Tom's phone stopped. Star hung up angrily. She should have gone with the handsome man. She missed him more than he missed her. Star realized her mistake in playing hard to get. She hoped he wasn't with another woman. Kissing the sexy man in public left her needy. She felt uncomfortable. She wasn't in the mood to take care of herself though.

Lin → "You strong ka."

Gai → "Want boom-boom ka?"

"Next time, Gai."

"Promise ka? Wery handsome ka."

"Nan, rub me meu sahy. Use left hand. Keep your right hand moving … meu kwah … switch hands. That's good. Yeah, Nan."

"Three ball hard ka."

"Keep going girls. Don't stop. Don't stop, even if I say stop. Kow jai mai ka?"

"Kow jai ka. Mai yut."

"Ka."

"Right, good. Keep going. That's great. Almost there."

"You so strong, MISter."

Tom arched his back. His heels and shoulders supported his entire body weight. He pointed his toes. He closed his eyes. He saw Star's lovely mouth. It was close. He opened his eyes. Tom sprang upright and formed a huddle, positioning their faces. His sudden aggressive action startled them.

"Stay there girls. Watch. Watch me."

Tom held their pretty Thai faces in place. The girls stared agape. He squirted. On each surge, he pushed them closer. The sniper hit his facial targets. He aimed by shifting their heads. The girls complained about their hair, noses, and eyes. He lost control, as he dreamed of Star.

When Tom couldn't bear the pleasure, he released his grip. He clinched his fists. He shook. They wiped their faces. Gai blew her nose. She coughed. The girls babbled about what they'd witnessed. Lin wiped him. He shifted his position. When the commotion settled, Nan increased the cooling power of the air conditioner. They were all sweaty.

CHAPTER 16

TOM STARED AT the masseuses' messy faces. They stared back, startled by his volume. The girls swallowed. They chatted about the amazing American. They giggled. Seeing their covered Thai faces gratified him. The next time he hoped it would be in Star's mouth. His breathing slowed.

"Remember, you promise me?"

"You need shower, MISter?"

"Uh, yeah."

The girls combed their fingers through their hair and wiped the captured material on a towel. Nan rubbed her fingers together. He grabbed his clothes. Attractive and horny Lin led him to the shower room, on the other side of the shop. The other girls straightened up the room.

"You want boom-boom?" Lin asked.

"Okay."

"Ka."

Lin spread towels on the floor and got down on her knees. She faced away. Tom kneeled. Reaching around, she guided him into her tiny hole. Only half fit.

"Hard, MISter. Quiet. Lin not want other girl know. Gai angry me."

"It'll be our secret."

"Ka."

Tom filled Lin. Although uncomfortable, she asked him to go deeper. She leaned forward on her palms. He pulled her thin thighs. He dreamed of kneeling behind Bpee. He tried to swap Star for Bpee, but the gorgeous ladyboy remained. His rapid thrusts drove Lin to ecstasy. She repeated "Me no think" again and again.

Lin squirted, while he dreamed of thrusting into Bpee.

"Coming again ka. Me no think. Me no think. Me crazy ka."

Lin jabbered. She became loud. She loved having the handsome American inside her. She hadn't come from intercourse for many weeks. In an effort to silence her, Tom wrapped his hand over her mouth and pinched her nose. The asphyxiation intensified her orgasms. Her face turned blue. He lifted her off the floor.

"I'm coming, Lin. I'm coming inside you. That's good, Bpee."

Tom slowed. He released his grip from Lin's limp body. She gasped.

"Lin no breathe. Mee khwam suk mahk, mahk ka."

"You felt good, Lin."

"You shower. No tell other lady ka."

"Okay, Lin. Our secret."

"Lin happy you come inside ka."

Lin hugged him. He felt shame for finishing in Bpee.

***

Lin disappeared. Tom showered. He used soap and hot water in an effort to remove the oil. She brought fresh towels. The air conditioner helped them cool down. He rubbed hard with a towel. He lost track of time. Star would be angry if he didn't call soon. Lin watched him dress.

"Lin, very good. Thank you. One-thousand baht for massage. Two-thousand tip."

"Korp khun ka. You pay other girl ka?"

"Yeah, I'll pay them on the way out."

"Ka."

Lin kissed Tom. They walked to the entrance. She limped, and her face was red.

"Long shower, MISter?"

"He, he, he."

"Oil's hard to remove. Water's not that hot," Tom blushed.

"Ka."

"Gai, one thousand for you; Tin, one thousand; Nan, one thousand. Lin, I gave you a thousand tip already. I paid Lin for the massage."

They smiled.

"Ka."

"Thank you, MISter."

"Remember, you promise ka. You promise came back ka," Gai said.

"Came back and see us."

"Anytime. You handsome man ka."

"Lin unlock door you ka."

"Thanks. That was great. I feel better. Much better. You Thai girls are amazing."

"Thai girl make good wife ka. Good take care ka."

Tin → "Hope see you again."

Nan → "Ka."

"Me too ka."

"Came back soon."

Lin → "Here number me."

Gai → "Remember, you promise me. Here telephone number me ka."

Tom took the phone numbers. They laughed and smiled. It was a big payday.

"Nan miss you ka. Miss you three ball."

"I'll come back for another octopus massage."

"Act toe … act toe … push?"

"Eight arms."

"Bplah meuk ka."

"Oh, bplah meuk."

"Bplah meuk is Thai for octopus?"

"Ka."

Tin → "Bye."

Nan → "Good-bye."

"Good-bye, girls."

Gai → "Bye ka. No forget."

Lin → "Ka."

Tom left Darling's Professional Massage and entered the maze of sois back to Baan Ketawa. He felt relaxed. His face locked in a big smile. He decided to wait, until he reached home, to phone Star. If she wanted to meet tonight, he wasn't sure how well he could perform. Given her sexy mannerisms, if necessary, he would rise to the occasion. The third ball made his recovery shorter.

CHAPTER 17

I'VE GOT TO HAND it to you, ole boy, you know how to enjoy yourself—an octopus massage. I heard of four hands, but never eight. I miss Thailand. I fix a glass of Maker's Mark. I open the file Part14Star.

After taking a drink, Tom called the bronze Thai goddess. Due to a change of heart, Star apologized. Being alone gave her time to think. She figured Doc was angry because she'd left him hanging. This explained why he hadn't answer. Her faulty logic meant he didn't need an alibi for the octopus massage.

In order to win his favor, and keep a watchful eye, Star suggested they go away for the weekend. Tom agreed. She would pick him up Saturday morning.

***

While searching online, Tom found a place in the Mae Sa Valley in the Mae Rim District of Chiang

Mai. At the impressive-looking Panviman Spa Resort, he booked three nights in a luxury pool villa. He asked Star to bring a swimsuit. In the lush setting, a man-made waterfall tumbled down a series of steps into a private pool, brushing water over its infinity edge. He couldn't wait to take her in the pool.

***

Star arrived an hour late. While waiting for the gate man, she texted Tom. He put away his laptop. He knew beauty required care. She's worth the wait. Tom tossed his bag into the back of her new, black, fully loaded Camry.

"Sa waa dii krap."

"Sa waa dii ka. You drive ka," Star stated.

"Sure."

When Star got out, she planted an uplifting kiss and gave him a warm hug. Tom was in like Flynn. As her tongue penetrated his mouth, she regained control over the rich American.

"Oh, that's nice. You're so sweet, Star."

"Bpak wan."

"You look amazing. Sooay mahk krap."

"Khun lor mahk ka."

"Thanks."

"Ka."

The bronze Thai goddess wore a skimpy yellow corset decorated with black ribbon, which threaded its way up the sides through gold grommets. The elegant garment levitated her curvaceous breasts. Her satiny-yellow miniskirt exposed breathtaking bronze legs. Her sexy yellow sandals, whose straps climbed her calves, matched her corset.

Star's fingernails were coated with a French-dandelion polish. A unique bronze-star galaxy, meticulously painted on each, indicated hours in the nail studio. The sandals revealed her flawlessly shaped toenails, which were painted neon yellow and shiny silver in various sizes of double-beveled knives. When she caught him staring at her toes, she knew what he fantasized about doing. He blushed.

With Tom behind the wheel, the attractive couple headed toward Mae Rim. Given her allure, he wasn't confident he could last 40 minutes. He poured compliments on her. Although jaded, she accepted them. She put a hand in his lap. He turned up the AC. She checked her look in the mirror.

The drive left the crowded and polluted city behind, and carried them into the winding mountain roads near Doi Suthep-Pui National Park. Outside Mae Rim, they passed a snake farm. Tom rebounded quickly from his heartache about Joy. Star didn't notice his detour.

Many tourist attractions lined the road, including go-carts, an orchid farm, a zip line, the Tiger Kingdom, a shooting range, a lepidopterarium, a crocodile farm, an art gallery, a wildlife sanctuary, a sculpture garden, an insect museum, and an elephant camp. Food carts, flower stalls, gift shops, hotels, gas stations, fresh markets, antique shops, 7-11s, cafés, traditional clothing stores, noodle shops, and fruit carts filled in the gaps. Tom enjoyed the scenery, while Star occupied herself in the mirror, putting on makeup, taking selfies, and fiddling with her yellow Chanel bag. When preoccupied with her beauty, he missed things along the way too.

"No underwear ka."

Star took one of his hands and placed it between her thighs.

"You're sexy. You're wet!"

"Me wery wet ka."

Star pushed in his hand, until his fingers arrived where she intended. While spreading her legs, she slid down. Her button's unusual size made him curious. He wanted to peek, but the narrow and dangerous road required attention. Tom considered stopping, the car.

When people stared and admired her beauty, Star's ecstasy heightened. She lowered the window. The AC struggled. She put her feet on the dash and made sexual innuendos to those roadside. Next time, she wanted them to finish inside their lovers, while thinking of her. Star's exhibitionism turned heads, as she moaned and came libidinously. Tom realized the cherry was her clitoris. It felt big.

Star played with herself in a supercilious manner, teasing Tom, until he finally turned off the main road.

"Almost there, Star."

"Ka. I close again."

"You're a naughty girl."

"Yes, I bad girl. Wery naughty ka."

"I see."

Star put her feet down and sat up. Tom realized he could never be angry with the bronze Thai goddess. She knew that too.

"You drive good ka," she smiled at her double entendre. "Me never come in car before."

Star lied.

"There's a first time for everything."

"Thanks for you helping hand."

"Starrrr. We park here?"

"Ka."

When Tom scratched his nose, he whiffed the bronze Thai goddess's perfume. His imagination ran amok, when dreaming about what was to come.

CHAPTER 18

A UNIFORMED EMPLOYEE waiting in the parking lot greeted the sexy Issarn girl and the muscular Navy SEAL. The small Thai man loaded their belongings into an electric cart and drove them up an incredibly steep hill. As the vehicle gained altitude and the view improved, the cart nearly overturned. Star clutched Tom's arm.

During the bouncy ride, Star's legs spread apart. The forced peacocking stimulated the self-obsessed girl, as did the thrill of no panties. The poser hoped another man would see. While resting his chin, Tom enjoyed the scent on his prognosticating fingers.

Their driver brought in the bags. He illustrated the functioning of the TV and AC, overviewed the restaurant and pool facilities, opened the minibar, switched the lights on and off, demonstrated the electric curtains, displayed the complementary robes, opened and closed an umbrella, explained the safe, and talked about the resort's other services.

When he began describing the spa, Star began listening.

Tom handled the paperwork. All he wanted to do was Star. As Tom's impatience grew, the bellhop sped up his spiel. Tom guided the man to the door. He nudged the dense bellhop. The man's face reddened. When Tom shut the door, the guy was still talking. Tom shrugged his shoulders.

At Star's request, Tom opened a bottle of expensive champagne. They toasted. He refilled. She opened her big, yellow Louis Vuitton suitcase. She pulled out a piece of yellow-nylon cord, handed it to him, and held her wrists out submissively.

"Take your clothes off."

"Tie me down ka."

When Tom went to close the curtains, the sexy Issarn girl stopped him. Star stripped obediently, hoping others would see. While enjoying her show, he removed his clothes. Tom wanted inside the bronze Thai goddess.

"Yai mahk. You wery big size ka."

"Thanks."

"Yai mahk, mahk."

Star's palm covered her open mouth. She feared the American would stretch her significantly. Any previous visitor would notice an unpleasant size increase. She made a quick decision.

"No boom-boom ka. Promise ka."

"What?"

"You yai mahk. Too big ka."

Tom ignored her. He didn't nod.

Reckless Star picked up the rope again. She teased and grinned seductively. She wound the cord around her hand and placed the coil in Tom's hand. This time he didn't put it down. He tied her wrists and attached them to the teak poster bed. The scarring on her wrists revealed a history of bondage.

Tom tested the knots. Star couldn't break free. Her depilatory cream kept her skin as smooth as Thai silk. He stared at her soft pink lips. She squirmed, and goose bumps appeared on her bronze skin.

"Please no ka. Please ka."

"You're in no position to make demands."

"Mai kow jai. Please ka. No boom-boom ka."

While gripping her ankles, Tom jerked Star into the middle of the bed. Her arms stretched. His rough nature unsettled her. He admired her stunning and toned body. He didn't agree to any of her demands. He would play the hand that he'd been dealt. Her worry set her hormones ablaze. With his spiking testosterone level, he fought to maintain control. He failed.

With arms overhead, the bronze Thai goddess's ribs stuck out. Tom ran his fingers around her orangey nipples. She writhed. Her natural breasts couldn't have been improved upon by surgery. In a rare victory, genetics won out over a medical procedure.

"Please don't ka. Don't come inside me ka. Please ka."

Tom listened halfheartedly to Star's pleading. He understood her, perhaps more clearly than she hoped. His lack of response troubled her. She started sweating. He cracked his knuckles. She stared at his six pack. Her worry intensified.

Their sexual tension built. To the bronze Thai goddess's chagrin, the Navy SEAL aggressively stuffed his underwear into the back of her throat. The choking sensation generated waves of panic, as her mouth was forced open wide. Deprived of speech, a distressed look swept across the helpless Thai beauty's face. While struggling to suck in air through her nose, she realized her big mistake.

Although Star cried out, only a muffled sound emerged. When Tom switched on the TV, her whimpers could no longer be heard. Her concerns amplified. Once back, he pinched her lips hard and used his other fingers to stretch her tight skin up toward her navel. This exposed her large, sensitive ruby.

Star's face showed acute fear. The breath-holding Navy SEAL began sucking. While circling his tongue, he went about his business as though eating an orange slice. He swallowed occasionally. Her kicking ceased. The bronze Thai goddess's legs bent upward involuntarily, as her juice was being drained. His strong fingers kept her in the wild.

Star wiggled. Tom swallowed again. She pointed her toes and shook. He lubricated himself with excretions from her effervescent lips. His baton would conduct her instrument in a booming symphony.

CHAPTER 19

IF THE BRONZE THAI goddess hadn't wanted the Navy SEAL on top of her, she shouldn't have provoked him with that cord. I open the file Part16Star. I'll bring it to the Nobel level.

To Star's horror, the giant American maneuvered himself on top. He paraded. The display intimidated her. The poor Issarn girl screamed, but his professionally placed gag restricted any intelligible noise from escaping. Nothing could stop the green-faced man from making her greatest fear come true.

Egged on by the look of terror in his captive's eyes, with one powerful slam, the Navy SEAL drove mercilessly deep inside Star's compact space, drilling her in defiance of her wishes. His violent insertion adjusted her attitude, when she realized she'd lost the game. She never would be able to lie about her virginity again.

As the Navy SEAL penetrated, he stretched the bronze Thai goddess's cylinder. Her spinning eyes, struggle, and flailing legs ignited his desires. He ravaged her once tight hole.

"I promise ka," he said smugly, with superiority.

Star's eyes shined in their sockets. The American conquered the incapacitated Thai. Distraught, she watched the powerful man pump her pampered body. The Navy SEAL raped the bronze Thai goddess, crashing mightily into her. He bashed her walls in an effort to make himself disappear. With hands pinning her down, his oxygen-starved prisoner couldn't move.

The Navy SEAL continued like a madman. He wanted to teach the game-playing Thai girl a lesson that her body would never forget. She stared at him moving in and out. He banged hard against her inner wall. When he reversed direction, she watched in horror, as her lips pulled backward. They rolled inward on his next thrust. Time slowed down. She couldn't believe something so long and thick was moving in and out of her body.

The green-faced man conquered her. Her lips rolled like dough. Her tears provoked a lunatic rage.

"This is what you wanted, isn't it?"

Star sprayed a milky fluid. Her farang-rape fantasy came true. A shock wave ran through her. Her contractions turned Tom into a lumberjack on a bucksaw. Her shaking encouraged his toppling her. He lunged back and forth. She lost control of bodily functions. He felt a warm liquid. In a fury, he dumped a colossal amount of semen inside the bronze Thai goddess. Fear spread across her face. As his third tank emptied, he gazed at her stupendous body. He shook to deposit the final pearly drops.

When Tom retreated, Star flinched. Her lips quivered. He glimpsed down arrogantly. If she wasn't on the pill, she would get pregnant. Her expression indicated she wasn't. The mighty man fell to the mattress. He chose not to remove her gag. This delay would calm her down.

Star had been getting insufficient oxygen for an hour. He pinched the Thai beauty's nose, until she kicked violently. As her face turned blue, she came again. The bronze Thai goddess was an emotional and physical wreck. He let her breathe. Tom removed his underwear from her lovely mouth. He untied her. Her red wrists proved she'd struggled valiantly.

"You finish inside me? Star come ten time. Me pee. Me poop."

They smelled her body's revolt. The maid had a big job.

"Star not want you come inside ka. You too big. Stretch me ka. Next time, me blow you. No boom-boom. Yai mahk. Me have baby. Me no want baby ka."

"Yeah, I'm sorry," Tom lied.

"Me worry. Me have baby ka."

"I understand, baby."

Tom's double meaning went over Star's head. Given her concern about stretching, he concluded she has another lover. He wondered how he could have been so dense. She drives a new car. She has an amazing wardrobe. She carries designer handbags, wears expensive sunglasses, and uses Louis Vuitton luggage. She wears a gold watch and uses an iPhone. She has a diamond belly-button ornament. She wears expensive earrings. He played with her hair.

The bronze Thai goddess's flawless beauty was responsible for Tom's actions and his love. He wouldn't let her go. He didn't care if she had another lover. He had many. He wanted to be with her forever. He wanted her to become his Thai wife. He made up his mind.

After regrouping, the young Thai beauty returned and forgave the American's action. She hugged and kissed him. Once he'd forced himself inside, she loved what he did. Star never lost control of her body or emotions. During intercourse, she never squirted, peed, or pooped. She never came so many times. While being penetrated, she usually didn't orgasm.

Uncharacteristically, Star worried about the consequences of her actions. Had she put them in danger? Would she get pregnant? Tom lusted totally for her. He missed her uneasiness. When the time was right, he would propose. He found a lovely Thai wife. He was in heaven; she was in hell.

Tom rearranged Caesar's famous words, "Vidi, vici, veni."

"Arai ka?"

Star raised her head. Her neck hurt.

"Nothing. Something some famous Italian emperor said. Well, kind of."

Tom grinned. Absorbed in troubling thoughts, Star didn't ask for an explanation. She had a lot of explaining to do. He stared at the ceiling and smirked at his rearrangement of the Latin expression—I saw; I conquered; I came. Pleased with himself, Tom took a drink of champagne.

CHAPTER 20

THEIR LONG WEEKEND at the Panviman progressed terrifically. The lovely Buriram girl taught the American more Thai, and he instructed her in American English. Although Tom couldn't master tones, he picked up more Thai than Star did English. Frequent mispronunciations resulted in hysterical laughing and goofy attempts and gestures. Their communication flowed with few misunderstandings.

Few farangs get the hang of Thai. Its tones are difficult. If you get it wrong, they'll have no clue. They're missing the context gene. We're missing the tone gene. Keep practicing. You have a beautiful tutor. I drink my Maker's. I get a throaty burn. It goes to my head.

As the bourbon washes my grey matter, I say, "Good job, ole boy." I continue my expert editing.

The bronze Thai goddess dressed up sexily for her American man in designer outfits, fetish latex clothing, and super-high heels. When they'd left, he never imagined the Louis Vuitton bag was a Pandora's Box. He enjoyed her surprises.

Star spent time styling her hair and applying makeup. She drew eyebrows long and wide. She wanted her tattoos redone, larger. Star glued eye lashes on that matched her hair color. The spoiled girl applied expensive creams to her uniformly colored bronze skin. Most Thai men consider women over 30 past their prime, and the Buriram girl feared wrinkles.

Star's clothes are bright orange, yellow, and red. Her heels match her outfit's color. Her makeup and clothing enhance the bronze Thai goddess's appearance. Tom understood that maintaining a perfect look required time and effort. He admired her and gave her the time necessary for beauty needs.

When exhausted from bedroom exploits, the couple opted for room service. If energy permitted, they ate in the restaurant. Other couples gawked. During daylight hours, Tom enjoyed the views of the Mae Sa Valley and its surrounding mountains. She took selfies. At night, Star twinkled. She took more selfies.

Star loved being treated like a princess, and in public, she loved hanging off the American's muscular arm. When people stared, her self-confidence and energy level soared. She's conceited. She behaves arrogantly. She needs pampering. She's a princess.

Star modeled her Brazilian, floss, bright-yellow bikini. She paired it with her high, yellow, fetish ballet-boots. The clear-plastic lower halves showcased her gorgeous toes. Her short-stepped walk and sexy sway drove him insane. She knows how to manipulate a man's hormones and make him desire her.

Whenever Star went outside, she donned a Japanese kimono. Tom realized she didn't want tan lines. He wanted great sex and to admire her unmatched Thai body. She wanted it to be evidence free. He kept his mouth shut about her charade.

***

When Star's phone rang, she needed to answer. She asked Tom to step out. It was another man. He didn't question her; he didn't want to spoil his vacation. When she retrieved him, her perfect appearance melted his heart. She pretended as though nothing had happened. He concealed his resentment. Grossly self-absorbed, she didn't notice any difference in his mood. Her sweetness and beauty dissolved his indignation.

Star turned on the outdoor, evening lights. Wearing her floss bikini and haughty attitude, she slithered to the pool. She turned on Tom with a striptease. After the call, dancing nude in the open made her feel free again. When she arched her back, her chest pointed toward the stars. She pinched her nipples and hoped a neighbor was spying.

Star pulled down Tom's swimsuit. She started. He became lightheaded. As she probed, she became fascinated with his testicles. He explained his polyorchidism. Star believed it related to his huge size. She thought he possessed magical powers. Star felt an urge to be watched; she began her performance; she wanted to be a star.

Tom stared, as her lips pressed outward. He took out his resentment about the unexplained call by driving hard into the back of her mouth. He gripped the sides of her head and forced open her throat. He thrusted. She choked. With handfuls of hair and ears, he controlled her movements. He suffocated the naughty girl.

Star's bony throat constricted him. She coughed. The asphyxiation immobilized her. Her eyes bulged. She didn't feel attractive anymore. She felt humiliated. When he came, he forced her to swallow. Her faced turned blue. Tears leaked from the drowning girl's eyes. She hoped no one was watching. She wanted to turn out the lights.

Tom blamed his aggressive action on the increased testosterone caused from his third testicle. Although Star didn't understand, after she regained composure, she seemed satisfied. She wanted the American to fall in love with her. Watching her choking went a long way toward his forgiveness, and satisfying his need for retribution.

The night was still young; there was more to come.

The couple rode a golf cart down the absurdly steep hill to Star's car. Tom drove them to a shooting range. With a rifle, the Navy SEAL impressed everyone. He set all-time high scores in every category. A crowd gathered. She fed on the attention.

Star selected prizes. She felt proud to be the shooter's girlfriend. Experts at the range figured he must have been a real sniper. His shooting ability is scary. The shooting gallery put the lovers in a horny mood. They hastily loaded prizes into the Camry.

Although the dark, mountainous roads demanded a slow speed, Tom threw caution to the wind. His screeching tires further added to their excitement, as they rushed back to the bedroom.

CHAPTER 21

I'M EDITING IN FILE Part18Star. I wasn't wrong about ladyboys. I need to learn to trust my instincts.

"MISter, you frog tattoo?" Joy asked.

Daniels pointed.

"Yeah, this? You've seen it before."

Ryan smiled. He stared at the young Thai girl's pretty face.

The skeleton-frog tattoo on her customer's chest reminded Joy of Doc. Ever since she'd lost her mobile, her life became miserable. Although she knew Doc loved her, and even thought that they would get married, she had no way to contact him. Chiang Mai is an impossible distance from Bangkok.

Joy realized that Doc couldn't contact her either. Their only link had been her mobile. Joy wished that she'd written down Doc's number. Although she'd spent hours searching for her mobile, she never found it. The hope of him calling, someone answering her mobile, and returning the phone to her had all but disappeared. She instead hoped that one day Doc would return to Lucky Massage. She prayed that he would return soon.

Joy went through her normal routine with Daniels. She squirted oil on his muscular groin. She squeezed him tightly and raced her little hands up and down, until he became hard. Then, Joy let him get on top of her. He never satisfied her like Doc did. He didn't have three balls. This American didn't treat her sweetly like Doc. He was more interested in finishing inside. They didn't have feelings for each other. He treated her like a piece of meat. When the man finished quickly, she felt happy. They never kissed.

***

Joy gave her customers hand jobs. The muscular American with the frog tattoo on his chest was the only man with whom she had sex. His tattoo reminded her of Doc. Because of the similarity of their tattoos, Joy figured they belonged to the same brotherhood. Although she wanted to ask the man about Doc, she never did. The man came by regularly, and perhaps one day, she would get the courage to ask him if he knew a man named Doc—a man with a similar tattoo.

The young girl from Surin needed money. She needed big tips. Once Doc's payments stopped, she was forced into providing sex massages again. She needed to support her family. She needed to buy food. Although Joy wanted to remain faithful, as she'd done initially after Doc had departed, the hope of him returning to Lucky Massage diminished over time. Her life went on as usual. Her dream of getting out of the sex industry evaporated.

***

Daniels became addicted to his sessions with Joy. He planned to continue getting a massage from her every few days. Her sexy little Thai body and skills satisfied him. He understood why Doc had fallen for the girl. Daniels didn't feel remorse about preventing her from going to Chiang Mai. He knew she was underage. In some warped way, he felt that he was even doing his green-faced brother a favor. He knew that his time with Joy could never be revealed to Tom. If Tom learned his secret, all hell would break loose.

***

Bpee's lifestyle had improved after she received the 50,000 baht from Doc. She wanted more, but she didn't want him to catch her in a lie. Bpee had feelings for Doc. She believed that if she could get him into bed, the two could develop a real relationship.

She needed to find a way to convince him to let her come to Chiang Mai.

Joy never connected the dots that Bpee's improved lifestyle was related to her missing phone. The ladyboy looked out for her own interests. She kept her secret. She did what was necessary to survive in Bangkok. One day she might try to blackmail Joy or her American boyfriend. Before she took that step though, she wanted to try and win the American's heart.

***

I, of course, never went with a ladyboy. I've already admitted to my prejudices. I tried to be open minded about them. But, Bpee's actions have confirmed my stereotype. Ladyboys are clever and conniving. I can't believe Bpee made up the story about the necrophiliac and Joy's suicide. She caused Tom and Joy great distress. Bpee has prevented the young lovers from communicating.

Joy is servicing Ryan Daniels regularly. I hope that Tom never finds out. If he does, I fear it could end the cyber operations in Thailand. That would be bad for the country.

I'm no better than Bpee. I'm deceiving Cam-Tu. I'm not really deceiving her. I'm not that bad. Although we're lovers, we never have talked about a long-term relationship. In fact, we never have talked about our relationship at all. We enjoy each other's company and our intimacy. These troubling times make us crave contact. I'm not in the same category as Bpee. I never stole anyone's phone. I never lied about anyone being

hanged. I never stole anyone's money. I never lied about anything.

It's good to know that Joy is alive. It's bad to know she
needs to service Daniels to survive. It was wrong of him to
prevent Joy from traveling to Chiang Mai with Tom.

CHAPTER 22

STAR DUMPED AN assortment of sex toys on the bed. She surprised Tom. Although the bronze Thai goddess wanted perverted things done to her body, she didn't want him inside her vagina again. Her rule upset him. She feared being stretched farther. If by some miracle she wasn't pregnant, she didn't want to take that chance again.

On seeing his anger, Star offered Tom her back-door. His size worried her. One of her fantasies was of a farang raping her from behind. While masturbating, she played that scenario out in her mind. That vision always took her over the edge. He relished in her alternative. She asked for it. He would comply. He would punish her. She deserved it.

From their initial meeting on the neighborhood soi, Tom never imagined the innocent bronze Thai goddess is such a kinky girl. Her deceptive behavior, coupled with her exhibitionist nature, boils his blood. They share a volatile chemistry.

Star pawed through the paraphernalia. She handed her strong American boyfriend two clamps.

"Put here ka."

"These are tight."

"This go inside. You come behind."

Star rolled onto her back. She began fingering herself. Tom set the first clamp. She grabbed the sheet. Her fingers kept busy, pressing strongly. She focused. Intense sexual stimulation released chemicals that increased her pain threshold. The first nipple clamp cleared her mind. Her masochist bent required the second one. Once attached, the connecting gold chain settled at the base of her spectacular bronze breasts.

Star pulled hard on the chain. She clenched her teeth. As requested, he pushed in the vibrator. It vanished. It felt much smaller to her. She recognized its steady hum. The Pavlovian whir excited her fantastically. Pain flowed from her chest into her shoulders and down her back. The suffering removed rationality. She wiggled her toes.

Tom flipped Star over onto her knees. His strength invoked fear. He positioned himself behind, between her legs.

"Put in mouth ka."

"I see."

"Behind only. No boom-boom front ka."

Tom didn't promise anything. He reached over with the gag. She opened her mouth. He pushed the ball in and fastened the collar's buckle. She couldn't talk. The restraint prevented mouth breathing. His aggressive handling excited her.

The muscular American applied K-Y jelly. When she felt his fingers, Star pulled down firmly on the chain. Her eyes rolled up in their sockets. The vibrator balanced out radiating chest pain. She anticipated his actions. He kept his hand busy.

Star contracted on the waltzing vibrator. Insufficient oxygen caused a dizzying ecstasy. She'd taken yah-bah pills secretly, and her heart raced. The combination of stimuli overloaded her senses. Panic engulfed her, and she convulsed. He turned her head with a handful of hair and slapped her. She tasted blood. She smiled.

Star envisioned a large crowd of jealous Thai men watching her, while she engaged in sex with the handsome farang. She imagined giving them each a turn, while he was forced to watch. The exhilarating visions produced an orgasm. Star stared straight ahead. She grunted; she shook. Tom marveled. She never believed a psychological orgasm was possible. She'd forgotten the vibrator—out of sight, out of mind.

Tom is surprised by Star's behavior. Most Thai women enjoy kinky sex. Issarn girls do. Many spend 12 hours a day in the sun in rice paddies. While bent over planting, there isn't much to do but think about sex, especially with only a grammar-school education.

Star's latex, canary-yellow, thigh-high boots exposed her bronze skin through the crisscross lacings running up her legs. Tom burned with desire. He needed to get inside the bronze Thai goddess. She balanced on her knees and elbows. The degradation caused by assuming this posture excited her further.

Tom scooted closer and admired her amazing body. He would do whatever he pleased. Star couldn't stop him. She braced. She cried out. She wanted to be heard. Her grunts dehumanized her. She never thought to remove her gag. Her mind wasn't working. The yah-bah played tricks. The helplessness and uncertainty triggered anxiety.

Star had offered to be sodomized. Although she had requested the forbidden act, her vulnerability troubled her. Her fear resulted in another thrilling orgasm. She tried to slow her mind, to stop the mental stimulation. The hidden vibrator kept her orgasms coming. Star swallowed. She couldn't clear her rape fantasy.

Tom gave the nervous, vulnerable girl what she'd requested. In a perfect storm of mental and physical stimulation, she screamed. Her pleas never got passed the gag. She'd put herself in this position. Electrocuted by ecstasy, the mixing chemicals sent her into freefall. She'd overdosed. He continued.

In an effort to regain control and stop her unbearable pleasure, and escalating fear, Star yanked on the swinging chain. She wanted to come down; she needed to come down, right then. She wanted an axe to break the glass. As he took what she'd offered, she struggled to balance. She forgot where she was, and who she is. She forgot who was behind her. With each contraction, a milky way ran down Star's thighs.

The Navy SEAL no longer cared what the kneeling, faceless girl felt. She'd taken her fantasy too far. He'd been in this situation before. He needed to come across the finish line. He channeled his anger into a rampage. He grabbed her hijab and went berserk. Losing all decency, the testosterone-saturated man gave her more than she'd bargained for.

The narcissistic girl thought only of herself. Her body jerked erratically, in an effort to make its rebel owner pay for the intentional sensory overload. Star's emotions bounced around in a tumultuous frenzy. Her capricious mind entered an unmanageable chaos.

***

The sweaty Navy SEAL finished round one. Star returned from a far-away place. She removed her gag and tossed the whizzing vibrator. Tom washed and switched holes, re-entering doggy style. She hadn't recovered. He moved with the intent of expanding her aperture. She blasted into space again. Her emotions shredded.

Unable to maintain control, Star stretched herself farther with violent thrusting. Her emotions did an about face. The bronze Thai goddess wanted him a permanent part of her constellation. She ignored consequences. She wanted the handsome farang to come inside. She wanted the rich American to get her pregnant. She wanted to be *his* wife.

Star ranted about being a bad girl. Turbulent visions circulated in her mind's tornado. Unmet desires spiked. Caught in a web of intense, mercurial emotions and mind-blowing chemicals, spinning wildly out of control, she went into a psychotic tirade.

Star talked about American men being rich and Thai men poor. She said she hates farangs because they're too good. Then, in contradiction, she swore she loves farangs. She professed her love for him. She asked him to hurt her. Over and over again, she talked about coming. She begged; she pleaded. She said she hated her family; she loved him. She demanded he continue. He continued. On the verge of a nervous breakdown, her cathartic rant escalated.

"Me love farang. Harder! Me hate Thai. Harder! Me hate fat Thai. Harder! Me hate farang. Harder! Me love you. I coming! Me hate. Me love. Please no more. Please more. Please no more. No more. More! Me sexy, me sexy. Sexy me. Help me. Hurt me! Watch me. Look me. Me crazy. Me fucking crazy! Farang, Thai, Thai, farang. Me lost. Me love gold. Boom-boom. Harder! Don't stop. Hurt me! Fuck me! Harder! Want to calm down. Want to come down. Need to come down. Ohhhh, please help me!"

As Star spoke in tongues, she accelerated her thrusting. During her breakdown, she cried and shook wildly. In combat, the Navy SEAL had been there himself. Over internal struggles, he'd lost his mind and job at the NSA. She flipped; she went insane. She went crazy, but a damned beautiful crazy. He said nothing.

Tom stared at Star's sexy boots. She contracted her interior muscles. Trickles of blood traveled along the chain and met in the middle. She lost it again. To subdue herself, she yanked on the chain. Nerve bundles ignited all over her hot body and merged in a raging inferno.

The Navy SEAL exerted himself. He used force to dominate the disturbed girl. Panic fueled her breakdown. He wanted to finish inside his insane Thai lover. Tom returned to the desert sands. He heard gun fire. He sweat profusely. He tugged on her hair. He looked around. No one was watching.

"I'm coming in you, you crazy bitch!"

"Come inside ka!"

Star spouted about coming. She came undone. She bit her lip. She tugged on the chain. The pain rebalanced the electrical signals in her brain. His physical intensity dragged her back to earth. Time slowed.

Star's absence seizure left her wondering. Tom would never forget the way the bronze Thai goddess had acted, or the things that she'd said. She took him on a magic-carpet ride. As her internal storms abated, the troubled Issarn girl calmed. She remembered her name. She remembered him. She remembered Chiang Mai.

"You wery good ka. You amazin' man."

"I'm a lucky guy. To have a girl like you is a dream come true. You took me to another galaxy, Star."

"Gal … gal a …"

"Another place, where there are millions of stars."

"Ka."

"You said some real weird shit, baby."

"Ka."

Star rolled onto to her back. She wiped drool and blood from her lips. She had no clue what had happened. Asking a question meant losing face, so Star remained silent.

As Tom removed the clamps, Star felt the brunt of her folly. She experienced a searing pain from ripped skin. Her behind throbbed. Her mouth ached. Her ears and scalp hurt. After exploding like a supernova, conscious thoughts flowed again. She had lost track of everything. Her fantasies won. She hoped she hadn't said anything too incriminating.

Star knew she would be held accountable. She would be interrogated. She ran her hands over her boot laces. There would be grave consequences to pay, for both of them. She would worry about that later.

"Need wash up ka. You come inside?"

"I did what you asked."

"Star need you. America man good ka."

"Thai lady better."

"Star love you ka."

"I love you, too."

The words escaped Tom's mouth.

Star is the lady for him. The gorgeous Issarn girl's extraordinary beauty won his heart. He loved their kinky sex. Whatever the issues were, including bizarre mental outbursts, the crazy green-faced man believed they could work things out. The bronze Thai goddess's passion exceeded his wildest expectations. On the battlefield, he never saw anyone fully recover from such a hysterical outburst, but she seemed to be back.

"Star love you naka."

Hearing Star's sweet declaration reinforced Tom's thinking. His search for a Thai wife was definitely over. He would wait for the right moment, and then pop the big question.

CHAPTER 23

ON THEIR LAST afternoon at the Panviman, the loving pair went down to the big pool with the cascading waterfall. Star wore her kimono. The pool's infinity edge pushed the surrounding tropical vegetation far away from the blue tiles. The Navy SEAL impressed the Buriram girl by swimming laps underwater.

"Doc li-eh tattoo. You frog ka. Swim wery, wery good. You li-eh Froggy."

"Yeah, I'm a frog man."

Star had no idea what a frog man is. Tom laughed. He had no idea what an Issarn girl is. Star laughed. They were enamored. He wanted to get married. She wanted his financial support and freakish sexual capabilities. She wanted to possess him. He wanted her love.

Tom enticed Star to enter the water in return for swimming lessons, but she rejected the idea because of her hair. He already made her work over-time. When they returned to the city, she would go directly to the salon. It was hers.

The bronze Thai goddess wanted to visit the spa. She knew it's expensive. Tom dried off. Star wanted a couple's massage. He went along. He enjoyed doing everything, and anything, with his gorgeous Thai lover.

Star chose a pair of attractive masseuses for a two-hour couple's massage. They spoke to her, and handed her a couple of plastic packages. She and her boyfriend needed to wear under garments. Star ignored their rules. She asked Tom to strip. When the girls returned, the beautiful Buriram girl and the handsome American were lying face down nude. The girls admired their clients' bodies.

Few rules are enforced in The Land of Smiles. Money rules. Laws are suggestions.

When a masseuse began covering them, Star reprimanded her. No sheets were necessary. The masseuses poured fragrant coconut oil on the backs of Star and Tom's legs, and the girls began a relaxing massage. He recognized the soothing background music.

The couple's outstretched hands clasped above their heads, and they enjoyed the sensuous and delicate touches of the young Thai girls. After an hour of working on their shoulders, backs, and legs, the girls asked the pair to roll over.

"You wery big, MISter," the shocked masseuse said inadvertently.

Star moved closer.

"He, he, he." Star instructed, "Go ahead and touch him."

Star took the girl's reluctant hands and placed them on Tom's erection. The masseuse's curiosity defeated her timid resistance. Fascinated by his circumcision, blue rivers, and overhanging hood, she began exploring. She made a fist.

"My hand size same ball you ka. Nee arai? You three ball?"

"Arai?"

"Him three ball."

"Star, can you please explain?"

"Ka."

In Thai, Star described his polyorchidism. She told the girls that someone as big as her boyfriend required three balls. She said he possessed magical powers. They listened, amazed. The other masseuse wanted a look. She leaned over and stared. Her hands remained by her sides.

"Touch him," Star instructed.

"Ka."

"Are you okay?"

"I want to watch," Star smiled.

"Neung pan ka. Neung pan she ka."

"She need one-thousand baht each ka."

"I'll do it for you, Star."

"Ka."

"You okay, MISter?"

"Yeah, good."

"Ka."

The girls marveled at his tower. Star assisted by squirting coconut oil all over his groin. She moved back onto her stomach and rested her chin on her hands. Star grinned. She raised her feet and crossed her legs.

Their four hands moved up and down in a synchronized and mechanical motion.

"Reo. Reo mahk ka. Fast," Star instructed.

"Ka."

At Star's urging, the girls sped up their four-hand, cylindrical tube. The bronze Thai goddess felt jealous.

"All the way to the top. Squeeze. Then all the way to the bottom. Do it together," Tom explained.

"Ka."

He adjusted their hands.

"Here. Squeeze hard, like this. Kow jai mai ka?"

Massage girl 1 → "Ka."

Massage girl 2 → "Ka."

The vain Buriram girl repositioned a chair. She sat down and started fingering between her gorgeous bronze Thai legs. She slid lower. Her exhibition excited the American. Using a long nail, she picked at her ruby. The masseuses watched. Tom ran his gaze over Star's tensed leg muscles and settled at her pointed toes. He fantasized.

"America man boom-boom ka," Star stated.

"Arai?"

The girls kept their hands busy and increased their speed. They wanted him to finish. Their hands tired from their long trips. Star stared.

"You okay ka?" Star asked.

"Sorng pan. Sorng pan she ka."

"Two-thousand baht each ka?"

"I'm okay, if you're okay?"

Without any arm twisting, Tom agreed to intercourse with the two young Thai masseuses.

"Me okay," Star answered, although she wasn't.

Massage girl 1 → "Ka."

Massage girl 2 → "Ka."

"Sahm pan ruam gan ka?"

"Ka."

Star agreed that her boyfriend would tip each girl 3,000 baht in total. The girls agreed to have sex with her muscular man.

Approaching an orgasm, Star slapped in between her glistening bronze legs. The percussion beat attracted everyone's attention. She flexed her toes hard. Star directed the first girl to strip and bend over the table.

"Ka, like that ka. Good ka."

"Ka."

"You're a sexy little girl."

"Ka."

Drenched in oil, Tom positioned himself behind the frightened girl and drove into her tense body. Star delighted in his forceful penetration of the half-willing, little Thai girl. The other girl watched in fear and waited her turn. They needed money.

When the girl yelped, Star laughed. She barked orders. She wanted him to hurt the little Thai masseuse. The girl's pain made Star orgasm. The more the girl whined, the more Star demanded from him. The masseuse's legs trembled. His quads burned. The other girl peeked through her fingers.

CHAPTER 24

THE NAVY SEAL followed the bronze Thai goddess's instructions and watched her provocative expressions, while he moved in and out of the teary-eyed girl. Star placed a finger in her mouth and compressed her puffy lips on it. She tasted herself. The humiliated masseuse was forced to watch, as Star mimicked his rhythm.

The girl's distress and moaning brought Star to a riveting orgasm. She loves being watched. Her exhibitionism started at a very young age. She became addicted to others giving her attention. She craves it. Ever since those early days, her sexual satisfaction became linked to how closely others observed her. She takes pleasure in manipulating people, seeing desire for her in their eyes.

The masseuse pleaded. She was falling apart mentally and physically. Star enjoyed watching. She gained vicarious pleasure. The more duress the girl was under, the more excited Star became.

"You look me. You look me," a moaning Star commanded.

Star's orders turned the Navy SEAL into an animal. When the girl's legs finally buckled, he withdrew.

"You come inside, MISter?"

"No."

She sighed deeply.

"You next ka."

Star directed the awaiting girl into position.

"Bend over farther. Lean forward. Yeah, like that."

"Touch your toes ka," Star added.

"You too big ka. You hurt she ka. Me small, MISter."

"Do it," Star shouted.

The girl reached down.

"Look at me wittle girl."

"Ka."

The Navy SEAL did what Star instructed. The girl covered her own mouth to muffle her screams. He detected a jog in her anatomy. The bend excited him wildly and caused enormous friction. The girl felt extremely uncomfortable, and she needed to poop. Ruthless Star encouraged him, and delighted in the flustered girl's despondency.

"Look me. Smile me, wittle girl."

The green-faced man's might defeated the girl. Her bowels let go. As the smell permeated the room, the embarrassed masseuse began crying.

"She poop ka."

Their eyes humiliated the girl.

"Her shit she."

"And me."

"Me poop ka."

"Look me, wittle girl. Look me, Doc. Look me, look me, look me."

"Her poop and pee ka."

Star's proclamations about her own ecstasy took Tom to an elevated state. He stared at the stunning bronze Thai goddess. She grinned mean spiritedly at the girl who had her American boyfriend deep inside. Star's jealousy mounted. She orgasmed angrily. The girl being violated watched; the idle masseuse watched; Tom watched.

The distressed girl begged him not to finish inside. Star instructed him to finish inside. She told the girl that her boyfriend would finish inside. Star stood up. Although about to climax, the Navy Seal decided to take pity on the little Thai girl. As he began to pull out from the girl's boomerang, Star rushed behind the retreating man.

The bronze Thai goddess lunged at the Navy SEAL's back. She sandwiched him between the distressed girl and herself. Turning herself into a battering ram, Star threw her weight into the American, creating massive friction. Ladyboy Bpee's image flashed before Tom's eyes, as he felt the force of Star's hips from behind.

"No come in me please, MISter."

The Navy SEAL imagined ladyboy Bpee behind him. He lost it. While overflowing Star's victim, he shook uncontrollably. He turned around. The girl grabbed the table. She reached down between her legs. Star looked at his face.

"You finish? You finish inside she ka?"

"Yeah."

Star laughed crazily and backed away. Tom stood up straight. He looked at the helpless girl.

"You come in me ka?"

The girl stared at her sticky hand.

"Yeah, I tried to pull out."

"You no come in me. Please ka."

"I did. I just told you."

"No ka."

She wiped her hand.

"My America boyfriend come in you already," Star said disdainfully.

Distraught, the young girl was in denial. Star became angry and explained in Thai what had just happened. She made the masseuse feel guilty. Star blamed her for having sex with her boyfriend. As the girl wept, the other masseuse tried to console her.

"My man finish already. Stop it. Clean up. You finish massage," Star barked.

The girls followed Star's orders. They washed Tom. They cleaned the floor. One sprayed air freshener. He couldn't believe they were going to finish the massage. The shattered girl eventually calmed down.

***

"Wake up, MISter."

With the massage complete, Tom tipped the girls 3,000 baht each. They happily accepted the money.

After receiving payment, one girl said, "Come back soon ka."

The other girl added, "Come again ka."

Tom smiled.

"Good-bye."

"Bye ka."

Tom held Star's hand. He shook his head. She frowned. They walked back to their room. Rather than rejuvenating them, their massage had drained their energy.

In the heat of the moment, Star acted out her kinky desires. Later, she regretted that her boyfriend came inside the cute massage girl. She recognized her mistake. He enjoyed being with that common girl. Star concealed her resentment toward him.

***

Tom settled their bill. He left a large tip for the Panviman staff who had the job of cleaning up Star's mess and washing the sheets. They drove back via the same route. She asked him to store her prizes from the shooting range. She couldn't risk bringing them to her apartment. He understood her situation.

Tom firmly believed that Star would sort her situation out in his favor. Her juicy French kisses, playful attitude, and peculiar sexual desires all convinced him. The coup de grâce came from her words.

"Me love you, dear. Me need and want you naka."

Star sought reassurances. Her fragile world, constructed on a foundation of material things, meant it could crumble easily. She needed him to say he loved her. She wanted his faithfulness and money, more than she wanted him.

When the bronze Thai goddess observed how much pleasure her boyfriend gained from having sex with the little Thai massage girl, Star believed that she'd lost part of him forever. Although he tried to pull out, she'd forced him to finish inside. Star held the American accountable for her actions. She could never truly love the American. He had disappointed her.

"I love you too, Star."

Star heard the words that she craved. They exchanged a long hug, but she acted out a role. She could never own him entirely. She wanted to derive the most benefit from him possible. In order to achieve her goal, she needed to dupe him. She needed to be convincing.

"See you soon ka," said a teary-eyed Star.

"Thanks, sexy. Thanks for a marvelous weekend. Will miss you. See you again soon."

"Love you ka. Good-bye."

"Love you too. Good-bye."

Chapter 25

A SECOND URN arrived containing my mother's ashes. I placed her on the mantle next to my dear father. When Cam-Tu entered the living room, she spotted the new urn immediately. She possesses a remarkable eye for detail. I feel she knows about Bim. When my mother's ashes sent me into depression, CT comforted me. I owe a great deal to her kindness, caring, and understanding.

Bim continues her regular deliveries and takeaways. Her free Thai sexual nature and desires lead us to experiment with new positions and activities. She's a tremendous amount of fun. While coming together simultaneously, we often laugh. I sometimes smile so wide that it hurts. I use her skills to supplement Cam-Tu's knowledge.

At first, Miss Nguyen didn't feel comfortable performing fellatio and swallowing, but under my tutelage and with practice, she's progressed and developed a great technique. She loves the feeling of me orgasming inside her mouth. More often than not, she pulls my pants down shortly after arriving. I make her a salty appetizer.

Ying Yue sends me both business and personal correspondence. I realize that her developing interest is based partly on my fortune and my prestige, as a Nobel recipient and a Distinguished Professor in the English Department at the United States Naval Academy. I'm not fooling myself. My parents had built me up as a great guy too.

Using her personal account, Ying Yue sends me provocative pictures; professionally photographed steamy nudes. She's trusting, and I'll never betray her. My Chinese attorney is lovely, and I desire her very much. She probably desires me too.

Even though I trust Ying Yue, I haven't sent her any images. I'm paranoid she might get hacked. I did guess the password to unlock *The Thai Wife Series of Novels*. Like politicians, professors shouldn't be sending around compromising photographs. I never will.

When I'm inside Cam-Tu or Bim's mouth, I think of Ying Yue's long, white legs wrapping around my head. This prevents me from hearing their struggles to breathe. It's selfish of me. After Miss Jiang releases her stilettos from behind my head, I apologize to my blue-faced girls for choking them. They recover their smiles quickly. They aim to please.

While engaging in intercourse, I visualize Ying Yue's Shibari-bondage photo. I can't get that image out of my mind, not that I want to. She sent it along with a picture depicting a bottle of coconut oil. I guess she wants me to masturbate, while dreaming about her—a thoughtful gesture, during COVID-19 confinement. Chinese-American women are direct.

Although I'm not using the image as Ying Yue intended, I doubt she would object strongly. When I slip into my Vietnamese or Thai lover, I dream about Miss Jiang. I feel like I'm with her. When I close my eyes, she's somehow closer. My actions feed off my thoughts. I have a great imagination.

I see the Chinese beauty clearly—not all Nobel laureates have such gifted recall—and I turn Bim or Cam-Tu into a bound Ying Yue. While inside Miss Jiang, I get excited with my girl. They have no idea what's going through my head. I'm not even sure anymore. It feels wonderful and real though.

I take a gulp of Maker's Mark. Although neither Cam-Tu nor Bim is here, I want to be with Miss Jiang. I grab a small towel. I reach for the coconut oil. Wherever she is, I'm sure she's smiling. I close my eyes. She's close.

The binding rope's satiny-black contrasts Ying Yue's white skin. The enji-red lipstick, the wooden Uchiwa bracketing the side of her jet-black bun, and the Akoya-pearl earring on her half-exposed ear make her appear Japanese. Her head turns to the side.

Down on hands and knees, with her feet floating in the air, the vulnerable Ying Yue rides on top of a red silk kimono. Her Oriental eyes look back disdainfully over her gorgeous white orbs, toward her magnificent shoes—made from matching blocks of Honduran mahogany.

The shoes' most striking feature is the back of the heel, which is a Takumi-carved circular arc. If the shoes descend, the white orbs fit exactly into the curvature of the backs of their heels. The craftsman designed the shoes to fit her spanking zone, as comfortably as they do her feet.

Ying Yue's teasing toes hide inside the sophisticated footwear. The pieces of grainy wood are ridiculously high and secured with confining red-Mulberry-silk ankle straps. There's a thin crimson-velvet decoration running along the tops of the shoes. The Chinese beauty's left ankle is adorned by a heavy silver chain, and that precious leg is positioned just behind her delicious right leg. Her ankles and pointed toes are at a pleasant angle to one another, so neither shoe is obstructed from my view.

The shoe on her right leg has its heel a tongue's length away from her mouthwatering moons. There are no blemishes or wrinkles on her porcelain, silky-smooth skin. Her long, delicate, white fingers have their nails painted a Ferrari red. Her rotated torso displays lovely fulsome breasts, delightful areolas, and cute nipples. The perimeter of the base of each caramel-colored nipple is dirty brown, while the areolas are cinnamon.

The glossy ropes spread her appetizing breasts apart and fill in her dainty cleavage, as the restraints ascend and bind her perfect shoulder blades. Her chin is resting on a piece of rope on her right shoulder. She doesn't seem to notice being tied up. The crisscrossing knots above her chest sit just below her exquisite neckline.

The lucky ropes also bind Ying Yue's curvaceous hips, and go between her milky legs, reaching up like a set of vines onto her creamy back. I see a blessed piece of black rope, pressing up inside her sweet, raspberry valley. Another lucky part brushes farther behind.

With Ying Yue's cherry-red lips pressed together, it almost appears as if she's blowing a kiss to her divine, bound orbs. Her wide and thin eyebrows decorate her alluring eyes, and her shiny sepia-colored eyelids form an elegant bridge between them. She has a symmetrical Duchess nose.

The shoes come frustratingly close to exposing Miss Jiang's toes, and the pieces of polished mahogany and red velvet leave me hanging, and guessing what her toes must look like. I imagine perfect little staircases. The brilliant master shoe craftsman erred in covering her toes. I get excited. The shoes force her toes to point.

On the cranberry-red wall, just behind Miss Jiang, is a glowing full moon. The moon's radius exactly matches that of the arc of her derrière. My hands have been busy. I hear YYJ whispering, "Come inside me please, my dearest Nobel laureate." I do, as she instructs. The Maker's Mark and my imagination have taken me on a trip to her moons and back. Thank you, summa cum laude Harvard Law School graduate Miss Ying Yue Jiang.

I open my eyes. I'm dizzy. I clean up.

Making love with Miss Jiang is a real delight. Starting with Bim, I'm thinking of asking if she minds me showing a slideshow of Ying Yue's digital portfolio, while we make love. Maybe I won't bother asking permission. If that works, I might try with Cam-Tu. Vietnamese girls tend to be more jealous. I should be careful.

Ying Yue's tantalizing photograph is the reason doggy-style has become my favorite position. I do want to take her from behind. But, for now, as the COVID-19 pandemic spreads, I'll satisfy my desires by dreaming of the Chinese nushen, when my other Asian friends are visiting.

***

I received a package from the Providence Medical Center, containing my mother's things from the hospital. Inside, I found a pretty picture. The receptionist, Ae-Cha Lee, signed the back and provided her contact information. Based on her appearance and name, I think she's Korean. If the photo is recent, she's younger than I guessed. She's really beautiful. I plan to send her a necklace, an autographed copy of *The Scorpion Girl from Issarn*, and my contact information. I hope we can correspond. I hope she contacts me again.

***

The coronavirus keeps us pinned down. I try to move on from the passing of my folks. I use the editing of *The Thai Wife Series of Novels*, Cam-Tu and Bim and Ying Yue, and Maker's Mark as therapies. I'm gradually approaching the end of the second book in the series, but there's no end in sight to the coronavirus pandemic. It seems to be going in the wrong direction.

Thailand is experiencing an increase in cases. The government is blaming the porous borders with Laos, Cambodia, and Myanmar. Since the junta took over in Myanmar, many refugees have fled to The Land of Smiles. Some of them were infected. Tak province got hit the hardest. I hate seeing images of the Thais turning back people who are trying to cross the Salween River. The pandemic and the collapse of democracy are a double whammy for the Myanmar people.

Tensions here are mounting over non-COVID-19 issues as well. Like poor Joy, everyone seems to be at the end of their rope. I haven't been outside for months. I re-engage with the file Part22Star. Although drinking, I won't let things get sloppy.

CHAPTER 26

I SOBERED UP WHILE staring at the Naval Academy's Chapel. I couldn't risk my writing dropping below the Nobel level. As a great writer, I take pride in my work. Critics are just waiting to pounce. I'm good to go now. There is much to tell.

The Navy SEAL and his Buriram girlfriend met frequently, and they enjoyed magnificent sex. She brought her bag of toys to Baan Ketawa and left some of her favorites. He took her shopping at Chiang Mai's malls. She wanted household goods. Before making a selection, she asked for his input. He thought she was preparing for them to settle down.

Tom bought the bronze Thai goddess tumblers, bamboo towels, a bed set, pillows, bowls, and silverware. They discussed the bed set and pillows at great length. She insinuated he would be sleeping on them for many years. She pushed for his opinion on the patterns and colors.

Ultimately, prices dictated Star's final decisions. She settled on the most expensive choice. He felt happy to buy the gorgeous girl whatever she preferred. Prices are lower than in the USA. He gave her the receipts. She loved being seen at the mall.

After shopping, they usually went to the movies. The clip about the Thai king intrigued Tom. It plays before every film and requires all patrons to stand. Out of respect, he removed his baseball cap, but Star always fiddled with her mobile. Others did the same. He knew the Thai song by heart.

Star doesn't enjoy reading Thai subtitles, so the Navy SEAL never saw anything with an English soundtrack. They watched Thai films. Although he prefers tragedies, dramas, and military films, the most popular genres in Thailand are horror and comedy. She loves to watch porn, but that is outlawed. So, they only watched it while at home.

Porn may be outlawed, but I'll never forget Thai sellers shoving it in my face in the markets at Sala Daeng in Bangkok. I understand that area is closed due to the pandemic. I wonder where all the salespeople went, and I wonder what they're doing now.

All movie tickets are reserved seating. Star prefers the expensive ones. From their VIP couch, Tom and Star ate popcorn. They cuddled in the theater. Sometimes, the brazen, bronze beauty went down on him. The private sofas are in the back. Most Thai people opt for cheaper seats near the screen. Star's exhibitionism astonishes him. He doesn't protest. She hoped to be caught.

The bronze Thai goddess hung all over her handsome American boyfriend in the malls, restaurants, bars, cafés, night markets, and streets of Chiang Mai. Star paraded him around. She wanted others to see her muscular, blue-eyed, rich farang. She thrives on people's envy. Being in the public eye with him, and never knowing whom she'll encounter next, thrilled Star.

***

The bronze Thai goddess required a few days alone. Tom didn't inquire why. Having flipped head-over-heels, he figured that she intended to break up with her other boyfriend. After she did, they could get engaged. Her absence didn't trouble Tom. The timing worked well, as he had a rendezvous with Pan and Wan at Baan Ketawa.

***

In a serious work session, Pan, Wan, and Tom ironed out the final details of the Ugly Gorilla operation. The girls gave the Navy SEAL the laptops. Pan coordinated directly with Daniels on the op and served as point. Both she and Tom assured Ryan everything was on track. Daniels updated Dr. Jones. All parties were on the same page.

Once they concluded their work, Tom melded in an out-of-this-world ménage à trois with Pan and Wan. Everyone enjoyed themselves. He didn't grant the ladyboy her wishes, but his inhibitions decreased. Wan recognized the developing bond between Tom and Pan. She was jealous.

Tom would have to put the brakes on his involvement with Pan if he was going to marry Star. He didn't feel guilty about his indulgence with his co-workers though, as he believed that Star was with another man. She was. She never felt guilty. She had a commitment to fulfill.

CHAPTER 27

THE NAVY SEAL double-checked his forged passport, reviewed his boarding pass, and confirmed that his secure mobile was in his pocket. Earlier, he'd loaded the latest version of the command and control software onto the two fake US-government-labeled laptops. He put them in his bag and included his personal mobile. Everything was good to go. He waited for Pan to pick him up.

Dressed in her Thai Airways uniform, Wan readied herself at the Chiang Mai airport and coordinated with Mae and a girl named Jum. Manow and Uan worked in support. Everyone checked in with Pan and confirmed readiness. She received confirmation that Ugly Gorilla and his wife had checked out of their resort in Mae Rim. They were on the way to the airport.

The details of the original plan had been modified slightly. Manow would be called planeside to escort Tom off the aircraft, through the jet bridge, and back through the terminal. Near the baggage-claim exit, Manow would hand Tom off to Uan. He planned to drive Tom to Salsa Kitchen on Huay Kaew Road. From there, the two would part company. Uan would check back in with Manow.

Pan and Wan would continue on with their flights as intended. No matter which laptop Ugly Gorilla's wife took, the couple would carry the malware back to Shanghai. If Ugly Gorilla brought the machine to headquarters, he would unknowingly infect their network and systems. The server back in the USA would begin receiving transmissions, revealing the activities of the PLA's main hacking group.

Pan arrived at Baan Ketawa 20 minutes early. She switched into heels. At the door, she gave Tom an inviting French kiss. After confirming the mission was on track, Tom was ready to depart. The lovely girl had other plans.

"Pan want you alone ka. Boom-boom ka."

Tom took little convincing. They stripped. Pan put her heels back on. She positioned herself at the sofa's edge and leaned over. Tom followed.

"I've wanted you alone."

They kissed. Pan turned around and guided him inside. She synchronized her gyrations with his thrusts. They integrated their bodies. She rambled. He listened. They continued.

"You're going to make me come, dear. Three, two …"

Pan looked over her shoulder and smiled at their perfect timing. The blue-eyed Navy SEAL captivated her.

"You complete me. We need to keep moving."

Tom jabbed into Pan a few more times. She smiled. They felt comfortable with one another. They cleaned up and got dressed. While he got ready again, she fixed her makeup and hair. She gave him a loving kiss. He reciprocated.

"That's nice, dear. You're special."

"Thanks."

"Okay, let's go."

CHAPTER 28

BEHIND THE WHEEL, Pan regained composure. Tom touched her leg. They flirted. Eventually, she turned left onto Loi Kroh Road. A minute later, she motioned at My Tee-Rak Bar. He glanced at the bar and saw a few cute Thai girls clearing beer bottles.

"You can meet me there anytime, dear."

"Thanks. Sounds good."

After an enthusiastic kiss, Pan dropped Tom at a nondescript soi off Changklan Road. She continued alone for their upcoming rendezvous. To remain incognito, he would arrive at the airport separately. Along the roadside to the Shangri-La Hotel, as he walked, his footsteps scared rats who were foraging in the gutter. The smell troubled him. In front of the hotel, he hired a quiet man from the row of tuk-tuks.

***

Tom purchased a Bangkok Post and waited for the arrival of Ugly Gorilla and his wife. He spotted Uan and Manow chatting. Pan lingered nearby. Wan identified Jum and Mae for the Navy SEAL. The security screener, Jum, stood at the entrance to a conveyor belt, and Mae worked inside. Tom guessed Jum was a late addition. He felt the presence of other operatives, moving about without his knowledge. Daniels wanted to ensure success and included backup.

A fat, loud, and greasy guy, wearing black spectacles, dragged his rolling luggage toward the security entrance. A leather satchel hung over his shoulder. A well-primped Chinese dish walked alongside. Her polished appearance contrasted the man's gut and unkempt manner. She carried a large handbag. Pan signaled the obvious. Wan headed through security to the gate. Uan and Manow watched.

Tom folded his newspaper and fell in behind Ugly Gorilla's lovely wife. She took notice of her pursuer's muscular physique and handsome smile. She returned a warm smile. The uncouth hacker took her by the wrist and pulled her closer. Pan followed.

With the lineup in formation, the four reached Jum's position in the corralled lane. Other passengers, mostly Chinese, went about their usual security screenings. Their kids darted about like prairie dogs, poking their heads up where least expected.

"Have laptop, sir? Mobile? Key? Belt? Liquid?"

"Uh, yeah. I've got two important laptops."

Pan attracted Ugly Gorilla's attention.

"Sa waa dii ka."

"You speak English?"

"Yes ka. How you enjoy Thailand?"

"Very good country. Pretty girls."

"Where you from, MISter?"

"China, maybe next ..."

Ugly Gorilla's wife understood English also, and she shot her husband a dirty look. Pan continued encouraging the sloppy man. Tom emptied his pockets. He sent his bag through, along with his mobile.

"Please place laptop in separate tray, sir," Jum said.

Jum assisted Tom in putting the laptops in their trays. The labels reading 'Private Property of the United States Government' were clearly visible.

Jum raised her voice, "I see you work for America government, sir."

"That's right, the government of the United States of America. Can I pass please? Those are very important machines."

"Sorry, sir. Yes, sir. Ka."

"Hello, madame. You have liquid, tablet, or mobile?"

"Just these," Ah Kum said.

Jum put Ah Kum's bag into a tray. She put the toiletries and mobile into a separate tray. They pushed the bins into the X-ray baggage scanner.

"Thank you. Go ahead, madame."

As the elegant Chinese woman passed through the full-body scanner, Pan fumbled with her things. She flirted with Ugly Gorilla. Enamored with the young Thai beauty, the PLA hacker became distracted. Meanwhile, on the other side of the conveyor belt, after the body scan, Tom flattered Ugly Gorilla's wife.

"You're very beautiful. You're not Thai are you?"

"No, I'm Chinese."

"Could I ask your name?"

"Ah Kum."

Tom hesitated for a moment.

"You speak English very well."

Ah Kum blushed. He touched her wrist gently. She smiled.

"Maybe another place and time. I'm sorry. I didn't mean to embarrass you. Nice to meet you. Hope to see you again."

"Yes. Me too. Thank you."

Mae slid ahead the bin containing Tom's bag. He collected his things, along with his paper. She pulled through the bin with the first laptop. She looked at Tom.

"Here, sir."

"Thanks."

Tom grabbed the laptop, loaded his bag, and headed inside the terminal. A flustered Ah Kum moved forward. Mae pulled the bin with the second laptop into place, as well as the ones containing Ah Kum's bag and other belongings. Ah Kum retrieved her bag and possessions.

"Here's your laptop, madame. Take it please."

The Chinese woman reached out her hand. Mae placed the laptop into it and let go. Ah Kum took the laptop. She looked down and read the label— 'Private Property of the United States Government.' Although her husband never shared his real work, Ah Kum knew he would want the laptop. She glanced around. She slipped the machine into her bag.

When Mae saw that, she directed, "Please move along, madame. Thank you ka."

Mae smiled. Pan crowded behind Ah Kum, backing up the queue.

"You holding up line ka."

Ah Kum went ahead. Pan collected her things. Mae signaled the plan was working. Ugly Gorilla followed Pan. While collecting his bags, he struggled with his belt. He thanked God this wasn't a security screening where one needed to take off shoes.

"See you on the plane ka."

"Maybe see you in Thailand next time too," the fat man tried.

"He, he, he."

Pan ambled farther into the terminal. She felt a reminder running down her legs.

When Ugly Gorilla and Ah Kum reunited, she scolded him for flirting. Knowing full well his intentions, she applauded her instincts and intelligence, especially in stealing the laptop. She led him into a quiet area and explained the laptop. She showed it to him. Her boldness impressed him. She accepted a kiss on the cheek.

Ugly Gorilla took the stolen laptop, read the label, and stuffed the machine into his satchel. In Chinese, he spoke in a serious tone to his wife, and told her never to mention the laptop again. She understood. He tapped her on the back.

Ugly Gorilla wanted to bring the stolen piece of US property back to China. If the machine contained important information, his status within the PLA would go up. A pay raise would keep Ah Kum happy. She attracted handsome foreign men. She was out of her husband's league.

CHAPTER 29

WAN SEATED TOM in business class and serviced him. Even in her mundane uniform, the ladyboy oozed sexiness.

"Bangkok Post, sir?"

"Thanks. I just read mine."

Tom handed Wan his paper.

"Ka."

Pan sat on the opposite side in the same row. Wan seated Ugly Gorilla and Ah Kum in front of Tom. The check-in girl had done her job well.

Wan suggested the Chinese man place his satchel in the overhead bin, but the hacker insisted on keeping it underneath the seat. Fooled by the gorgeous ladyboy, he ogled. Ah Kum glared to keep her husband in check. In protest, with mouth agape, he raised his hands as though about to perform a military press. She lowered his hands. He knew what he'd done wrong. Pan enjoyed Wan's performance. Tom shook his head.

Wan served Tom, Pan, and Ah Kum mimosas. The fat man perspired. He drank water. Wan kept his glass full. Tom surmised that the hacker's status in the Chinese government is what had won him such a desirable woman. The pilot and head steward ran through their usual spiels. Just prior to the boarding doors closing, Wan discreetly cued Tom.

"Miss, I forgot my laptop at security."

"Sir, boarding door closing ka."

Tom undid his seatbelt.

"I'll have to run."

"No time, sir. We send someone ka."

Ugly Gorilla pushed his bag farther beneath the seat.

"You don't understand. I need that laptop."

"I sorry, sir. Not possible ka."

Tom sprang up angrily. He slammed the overhead bin. Passengers cooed. Ah Kum raised a hand to her mouth. Pan watched.

" 'I sorry.' You don't even speak English correctly! I told you that's a very important laptop. I work for the US government. I must get that machine!"

"I sorry ka."

Wan's head drooped. Tom slapped the overhead bin again. She jumped.

"Listen to me! I know you ladyboys. You pretend to be women. You get hired because of your looks, not your brains. You're not hearing me! I must get off and get my laptop. Do you understand me? I don't think you do."

"Ka. I sorry, sir. No time ka."

"Are you even listening to me?"

Pan nodded to Wan. Another stewardess appeared. Manow arrived at the boarding door. Tom moved toward the exit. Manow pointed. Ugly Gorilla thought about Wan. He stared.

"Khon nee krap?"

"Ka. Him want get laptop, at security ka. Him angry me ka."

"Sir, please calm down."

"You miss flight, sir. Please return to your seat ka. I sorry ka."

"I don't care if I miss the flight! What do I have to do to make you people understand?"

Tom pounded the overhead bin. He frightened passengers. Ah Kum stared at the powerful man.

"Please be seated, sir," a stewardess said.

"I sorry ka."

"Please, please," Pan said.

She cued Manow. He grabbed Tom's arm.

"Don't touch me! I'll be back."

"I sorry, sir, you miss flight ka."

"I'll run then."

"Sir, please come quietly."

"You people!"

"Take all belonging, sir."

"I've got everything, but my damn laptop!"

Ugly Gorilla and Ah Kum watched. She became aroused by the handsome man's determination. The laptop's value soared.

"We see you next flight, sir. I sorry ka."

"I sorry. I sorry. Don't worry about me, boy! I don't care about the next flight. If I don't get that ... oh, forget it."

"Sir."

"Keep walking."

"Okay, okay. I'll do it on my own."

"Krap."

Ah Kum craned, as the man was escorted away. He disappeared from view. Ugly Gorilla breathed a sigh of relief. Ah Kum took a drink. Pan fastened her seat belt. Wan went to the bathroom.

After an announcement in Thai, the pilot followed it with his English translation, "Board door close. Flight crew prepare depart. Please take seat krap. Our fly time Kunming today one hour and twenty-five minute. We expect smooth ride. But, for you safety ..."

Pan observed the Chinese couple congratulating themselves. The Navy SEAL's remarks had hurt and embarrassed Wan. She needed to pull herself together. She snuck a mimosa. Wan had detected something special going on between Pan and Doc. Wan has strong feelings for him. Although the Navy SEAL's insult was part of the plan, she couldn't let it go.

Ugly Gorilla made advances at Pan. Ah Kum wanted to get drunk: to celebrate her victory and to tolerate her fat and ugly husband. She wished the handsome stranger was still onboard. Ah Kum dreamed about having the physically fit man on top of her. She hated having her fat husband on top. She drank.

When Pan felt another dribble running down her leg, the memory brought a smile. She took a drink. She admired Ah Kum. Her porcelain skin resembled that of the women in Osaka. Ugly Gorilla thought Pan looked at him. He returned her smile. Pan stopped admiring Ah Kum.

***

Manow led Tom in the direction of security. He waved discreetly at Mae and mouthed a 'thank you krap.' He hoped they would have a chance to meet again, where he could thank her properly. Jum had left her station.

Manow and Tom emerged near the baggage claim. As they exited, Manow handed him off to Uan. He escorted Tom to the front of the international-terminal building, where his police motorcycle was waiting. Tom decided to go to the Shangri-La Hotel. Although a minor deviation, he felt it more secure. After backslapping, Uan and Tom departed. On his walk to the Méridien Hotel, Tom recognized some of the same rats. The smell, if anything, had gotten worse, as the temperature increased.

Along the route, willing girls from massage shops propositioned Tom. He ignored their best efforts. When he entered the Latitude Bar, he took the same table as before. While cooling off in the AC, he ordered a mimosa. Tom texted Daniels about the drop's success.

A much-relieved Daniels, who had just come from Lucky Massage, congratulated Tom. They would keep in touch. Daniels informed Dr. Jones about the success. Tom received a big thanks. Mae texted him, 'thank you ka,' confirming she'd read his lips. Along with the mimosa, she put a big smile on his face.

Tom felt pleased to be back in the game and doing something useful for his country. Although a lot had transpired already, the day was still young. The Navy SEAL ordered another mimosa. At that same moment, Pan received a refill from Wan. While Tom sipped, he thought about the women and ladyboys of Thailand. Maryland couldn't compete. He felt happy to have been sent away.

CHAPTER 30

I TRIED TO CUT *back on my Maker's Mark consumption. I failed. There's so much bad news about the coronavirus everywhere. Everyone in The Land of Smiles is cooperating with the government's policies: wearing face masks, social distancing, and remaining at home to the extent possible. I don't really think they have a choice.*

The Thai government took Draconian measures. They set curfews, locked down, and limited inter-province travel. The protests against the military have lessened. Gatherings of more than five people aren't allowed. Many businesses have closed. Others are failing. I hope their strategy doesn't backfire and destroy the Thai economy. They're dependent on tourism. I hope Thai Airways doesn't go bankrupt.

Thailand's population is 67,000,000. They've had 3,000 cases and 50 deaths. The five-fold larger US has had 1,000 times as many cases and 2,500 times as many deaths. I'm concerned about Bim's activities, but I don't worry too much about Cam-Tu. I'm not taking any chances. I stay inside; I edit; I write. That's what Nobel laureates in literature do. We write. I open the file Part26Star.

With Star gone for a few days, the mimosas planted the idea of casing her apartment into the Navy SEAL's head. Although she hadn't told him her address, Tom knew it. Her apartment is in a new condo off Huay Kaew Road, not too far from Darling's Professional Massage. Like most condos in Thailand, her complex has a low-occupancy rate.

Many condos in Thailand are built for the purpose of laundering money. Corruption and the drug trade mean powerful people have excessive amounts of cash. Until electronic currencies get a foothold in The Land of Smiles, the safest way to hide millions is in new construction. A friend of mine in Bangkok was the only one living on the 14th floor of her building.

After leaving the Latitude Bar, Tom stopped by his place. The Navy SEAL dropped off his laptop. He picked up tools and surveillance equipment. Once finished at Star's room, he intended to stop by Darling's Professional Massage and come good on his promise to Gai.

***

Tom brought along a jammer—a device to prevent security cameras from recording. When he entered the bronze Thai goddess's condo complex, he switched it on. The poor angles of the cheap security cameras meant he probably didn't even need the jammer. He shook his head.

As a farang, Tom bypassed the usual lack security controls with little fanfare. He took the elevator to the top floor. It contains a handful of rooms. The lift was empty, as was Star's floor. He looked around. There were no security cameras. Tom located her door. He knocked. There was no answer. He smirked. The place was dead.

Tom easily picked the cheap lock and entered Star's spacious, penthouse apartment. He shut the door and locked it. Tom looked around. Her benefactor was obviously rich. The white, tiled floors gave the place a clean feel. Things were neatly arranged. On the walls hung Buddhist art. To his surprise, Star displayed his gifts.

The tumblers sat on a teak rack. The silverware they'd selected completed the place settings at the table. In the bathroom, their bamboo towels hung. Their bedding was on Star's bed. He prayed that she had a generous allowance. Tom exhaled forcefully, looked down, and shook his head. He entered her closet.

While browsing Star's collection of heels, Tom became aroused. He picked up a pair of boots and sniffed. The bronze Thai goddess is kinky. Dozens of pairs of stilettos and boots lined the floor. Corsets, tank tops, panties, school-girl uniforms, and bras filled the shelves. He found packages labeled 'Fetish Full-Body Cover.' He stashed one in his bag. He grabbed a pair of nylon stockings. Star wouldn't notice.

On the nightstand, the Navy SEAL saw a picture of Star with a rotund Thai man. Tom's heart sank. The bronze Buriram goddess towered over the guy. The fat man's expensive suit and gold jewelry indicated he could support a pretty girl. Tom hated the man. He slammed a fist into the bed. His future wife was the lover of a repulsive suit.

Having confirmed his worst nightmare, Tom collected himself. He snapped a picture of Star's benefactor. He heard a noise. It turned out to be nothing. When heading through the kitchen to the door, Tom noticed a wooden block stabbed full of knives and a meat cleaver. While shopping at Robinson's, he'd offered to purchase this identical, expensive chef's kit for Star. She'd declined without offering an explanation. He shook his head.

Tom slipped out of Star's apartment. He didn't feel well; he felt hurt. Once outdoors, Chiang Mai slapped his face. In the heat and humidity, red car and tuk-tuk drivers honked as they passed, hoping to pick up a farang customer. Tom ignored them and texted Gai. If she was available, he wanted her. She was free.

Tom walked briskly toward Darling's Professional Massage. Soliciting drivers continued their annoying cacophony. Gai fantasized. She pranced around the shop on her tippy toes, anticipating her massage with the strong, attractive American. In addition to a good payday, she hoped meeting him might result in a long-term relationship.

When Tom arrived, cheery Gai greeted him. They exchanged smiles. He looked more handsome than she remembered. She adored his blue eyes. He has a wonderful smile. Gai felt lucky. The green-faced man wanted to use her little Thai body for retribution.

CHAPTER 31

GAI LED TOM BY the hand.

"No other girls at the shop?"

"Them go temple. Shop wery quiet. Turagit mai dee ka."

"Tur … tur a …?"

"Turagit mean business ka."

"Sorry to hear business isn't good."

"Gai lone ka. Me lock door. We go back room ka."

"That sounds good."

"You bag ka?"

"Uh yeah, this. I have something for you."

"Weally?" Gai beamed.

"Krap."

When they entered the room, Tom pulled out the full-body cover.

"A gift I stole for you."

"He, he, he. You sweet man ka. America man good. Korp khun mahk naka."

"Open it, Gai."

"Ka."

"I don't need massage."

"You want boom-boom?"

"I promised. Remember?"

"Ka."

Gai became excited.

"Try that on."

Gai took off her clothes. Tom admired her perfectly proportioned little Thai body. Rifling through Star's apartment had left him edgy. The heat had sobered him up.

"You're small, Gai."

"Ka."

Tom tore open the package, and Gai removed the garment.

"Go ahead. Put it on."

Gai scratched her head. Tom refrained from laughing.

"Nee arai? Me confuse ka."

"Let me help you."

Tom unzipped the back.

"Me confuse mahk, mahk ka. Sorry ka."

"This covers your body and face."

"Weally?"

The fetish cover required rear entry. He helped the puzzled little masseuse enter.

"This funny ka. Gai never see same ka."

"That's good. Push your arms through. Yeah, like that."

"Me in bag ka."

Gai sweat. Tom helped by pulling the tight fabric over her skin, just as he did his wetsuit before a dive. Covering her hair and face, running all the way down to her feet, the garment formed a cocoon. Once zipped, the only exposed part of her body was where Gai had crawled through the entrance. She wiggled her fingers into the mitts. She had no dexterity. He pinched and pulled on the fabric, removing wrinkles.

"Me no feel good. Me worry ka."

Tom wasn't sure what she'd said.

"You're okay."

"Me no see."

The binding fabric restricted Gai's breathing. Every part of her body was being squeezed in the tight shell. Claustrophobia paralyzed her. When she opened her mouth to speak, Tom saw her lips pressing outward. Her muffled sounds were indecipherable. She wanted to escape the pliable trap.

Gai struggled to breathe. Her nagging, incomprehensible sounds agitated Tom. He felt like a pupa was prattling him. He stripped. The only available position was doggy style. Exasperated at Star, he pushed Gai's face down onto the mattress. He stared at the small opening.

The fetish cover rounded Gai's form and eliminated extremities, stripping away her humanity. She flailed. The bag poked out in random directions. Her contortions reminded him of the cobras in Bangkok, unsuccessful in escaping their master's burlap sacks. When Joy's horrible death entered his thoughts, his anger amplified.

As Gai slithered, Tom grabbed the rear entrance. He unzipped it a bit. She fell on her chin. With club hands and restricted hearing, unable to turn, her panic escalated. As a child, Gai's parents had punished her by locking her in a closet. That trauma returned. There was no air flow. She sweat profusely.

Bound, incommunicado, and confused, the helpless girl trembled. Gai's anxiety caused a debilitating panic attack, she wanted to flee. She tried to flap her arms. She could hardly move. Her mouth dried from excessive swallowing. She needed to break free.

While fantasizing about the gorgeous ladyboy Bpee, Tom made use of the coconut oil. He smiled at his busy hand. Gai wobbled in her kneeling position. She hyperventilated in her emotional nightmare. Hot, distraught, and struggling for air, her inhalations accelerated. Her dry mouth caused an overwhelming thirst. She needed a drink.

Unable to flee, Gai's shallow, rapid breathing triggered a desperate flight response. She needed to run fast and far. She couldn't move her feet though. Gai spit up. She felt the salvia against her face. She closed one eye. She was frantic, hyperventilating.

The Navy SEAL took full advantage of the helpless masseuse. He followed his ladyboy fantasy. He saw all of Bpee. He exerted himself for a long time. Gai went on a record-setting streak of orgasms, until finally passing out. When he withdrew, her limp body fell forward.

While Gai lay unconscious, the Navy SEAL showered. She was just coming around, as he finished dressing. He unzipped the cover. With his help, she emerged from it drenched. Her hair was soaked. Tom gave the dehydrated masseuse a bottle of water. He crumpled up the kinky suit. She wiped her face. She staggered.

"You amazin' man. Gai love you ka."

"Umm, thanks."

"You shower?"

"Yeah, you slept."

"Gai pass out ka?"

"You slept well. Glad you're awake now."

"Ka."

Gai took a drink. She kissed Tom. He thought his actions required a jail term, not a loving kiss. After their hardcore session, while unconscious, she'd fallen in love.

"You're amazing."

"Come see me every time ka."

"I'll definitely come back."

"Ka."

Gai's love overwhelmed her. The handsome American transported her to a realm she never knew existed. Her loss of consciousness symbolized true love. He held a deep meaning. Like many in her country, she believes her fate is controlled by an un-explained mysticism.

Gai believes that something from somewhere delivered this customer to her for a special reason, and she planned to take full advantage of it. Her good luck meant that she should buy lottery tickets. She didn't want to miss her opportunity. The fortu-itous timing of his visit wasn't simply good fortune. It was divine intervention.

Gai would do anything for her American man and to experience those out-of-this-world orgasms again.

Chapter 32

THE NAVY SEAL settled into a daily routine of walking to Chiang Mai University from Baan Ketawa. He learned that the locals call the university Mor Chor. When Tom needs fruits or vegetables, he buys them on the way back from Cat's stand. The quality of her produce didn't always measure up, but he felt indebted.

The matchmaking mother talked about Ket, describing her accomplishments, activities, and travels. Cat showed him pictures. Tom always feigned an interest. The two became friends. Although Cat's persistence increased his curiosity, he didn't want to give her hope. Contrary to his wishes, Cat's aspirations for Ket were increasing, not diminishing.

Per Dr. Jones's instructions, Tom established himself at the university. He met a group of professors in the Computer Science Department and a handful from Computer Engineering. Nearly all the lecturers, professors, and administrators at Mor Chor are Thai females. The demographics differ markedly from those he's accustomed to in the United States.

Most university women in Thailand come from wealthy families and don't need to work. The meager salaries don't trouble them, as they already possess enough resources to support themselves and their families for the rest of their lives. The prestige associated with a university job carries more value than the paycheck. The flexible schedule helps women who are starting their own families.

A male provider can't support a family on a measly graduate-school stipend. And, once working full time at a university, the 1,000-dollar monthly salary isn't sufficient either. Student loans come from the Thai government. Thai teachers and professors run up huge debts that they can't pay off. The majority of Thai educators with credit problems are male.

Tom hit things off well with Gam—an associate professor of computer science. She works in computer security too. Although much of his work is top secret, he could talk about unclassified material. Gam wants to learn from him, and she recognized immediately that his expertise is a great opportunity to advance her career.

Gam teaches on Monday, Wednesday, and Friday. She invited Tom to her office on Tuesdays and Thursdays. Her PhD dissertation addresses layered-network security models, and Tom happily discussed those with her. She proudly shared her work. He supported Gam to the extent possible.

One day, Gam's Thai PhD student, Mim, stopped by for advising. She'd completed all her coursework and was searching for a dissertation topic. The beautiful girl attracted Tom's attention. She's from Mae Hong Son—the mountainous province west of Chiang Mai. She was in her early twenties. Things between them progressed rapidly.

Tom started advising Mim. She wants an American boyfriend. While at home in Mae Hong Son, she only met farang backpackers. They don't interest her. As someone working on a PhD, Mim wants a well-educated partner. The blue-eyed, muscular American checked all the right boxes. She fell head-over-heels for him.

As Tom continued advancing Gam's research, she expressed no concern about Tom's developing relationship with Mim. The three of them would often gather for coffee. Gam mentored Mim a couple times per week. Since Tom started coming around, Gam actually saw more of her student.

Mim matured quickly. Accompanied with her growth came improved performance. Her increased capabilities helped Gam too. The developing situation was a win-win for all parties. Things at the university progressed in the manner that Tom's team had hoped. Daniels and Dr. Jones were pleased with his work.

Tom befriended Porn Katawatanawong, who works for the Thailand Fulbright Foundation in Bangkok. While Porn was visiting Mor Chor to recruit Fulbright applicants, a colleague at the university introduced them. They got along well. Porn suggested he visit her in Bangkok.

While in Bangkok, Tom would help review Fulbright proposals and provide input to the program. Porn requested his business card. He told her they were still being printed. She gave him a card and requested that he contact her. He agreed. When he returned to Bangkok, he planned to meet Bpee and investigate Joy's suicide.

***

Once Tom started receiving love notes from Star again, she wrote about her availability. Tom purposely missed her calls. His absence generated a flurry of sexy messages from the bronze Thai goddess, professing her love and desires. When she sent graphic photos, he finally caved in.

Tom's heartthrob is irresistible. He desired her immensely. He can't resist Star. His game of making her jealous was over. He'd succeeded in making her believe that he was truly angry, but because of her amazing looks, he never fooled himself.

***

After several fervid and fiery bedroom sessions, Star and Tom's relationship got back on track. With everything going well again, the attractive couple spent time together shopping and dining out. His situational awareness increased, realizing their relationship might be putting him in significant danger. He knew what her sugar daddy looked like. The bronze Thai goddess never considered Tom's personal safety.

Star pranced around everywhere in the city with her American hunk. She kissed him; she held his hand; she hung off his arm. Tom became concerned about being in the open with her. He wanted to avoid a public confrontation with her fat, businessman boyfriend. An encounter would compromise his cover, and worse, perhaps endanger his life. He couldn't afford unwanted attention. He couldn't afford to be murdered.

Tom learned that the bronze Thai goddess worked at a makeup and hair salon. Star graduated from a beauty academy, which helped to explain why she always looked so perfect. Her businessman boyfriend owned the salon. He let her go in and primp, whenever she wanted.

Although an employee, Star never attended to customers. The staff attended to her. Whenever she needed money, she took it from the register. In this way, she dictated her own salary. Her fantastic looks advertised the shop. Thai girls flocked to it, hoping to become as attractive as Star. Her aloof attitude attracted pretty girls.

***

At times, Star became distant to Tom. She excused herself to answer what she termed important phone calls. Overall, their relationship worked. He purchased her new clothes, shoes, and anything else she desired. He always paid cash, which impressed her. She always kept the change. He accepted her greedy behavior.

Whenever Tom went to SIAM Commercial Bank to obtain cash, the girls working there offered their numbers to him. In addition to his good looks, they could see his bank balance. Despite the mounting distractions, Tom decided that if things progressed well with Star, he would pop the big question. Fallback positions sprang up everywhere with no effort.

***

Tom received good news from Daniels that the team opened a data channel out of Shanghai. As expected, Ugly Gorilla brought the stolen laptop back to PLA headquarters. They successfully infiltrated APT1, and all sorts of valuable information flows out of Shanghai to Dr. Jones's home setup.

The US cyber-security team learned about China's intentions in the South China Sea. Critical information flowed in about the Philippines and North Korea, as well. New dirt emerged on Kim Jong-un and his sister. Dr. Jones even heard about the Chinese's problems in Venezuela, Hong Kong, and Iran, and with Putin. The PLA is casting a giant world-wide net in a massive economic grab. The team struck a rich vein.

Although too early to act, Dr. Jones was extremely pleased with the information being gathered. Tom and Ryan were given credit for the success of the operation. The Thais on the team received positive recognition. Dr. Jones wanted Tom to work on discovering zero-day exploits for PDF files. They planned to do some spear fishing using the names and email addresses being flushed out of their Shanghai data stream.

Tom thought about Ah Kum. If China detected the USA's malware, he wondered what her fate would be. Would Ugly Gorilla take the fall? Would she be incriminated? Tom couldn't imagine Ah Kum sleeping with her husband. The thought repulsed him. If the PLA sent Ugly Gorilla back to Chiang Mai, Tom hoped she would be tagging along.

Dr. Jones wouldn't allow Tom to go to China. The Chinese keep careful records of all US visitors. Tom wanted a chance to meet Ah Kum again. Because she was married to one of the Chinese government's top hackers, that presented a host of issues. Tom wondered about her line of work. She'd impressed him.

Daniels kept in touch. He assured Tom something big would happen soon. Their intelligence revealed the name of a rich Thai businessman with connections to the Thai Navy. He'd been selling top-secret information to the Chinese. Dr. Jones wanted the spy eliminated.

The spy's frequent visits to Chiang Mai meant that Tom might play an important role in silencing the traitor. They were close to securing a photo of the man. Tom's team were on high alert. Once the man was identified, they would need to move quickly.

CHAPTER 33

WITH YING YUE'S diligence, I tied up loose ends of my parents' estate. I retain her to pay bills, manage properties, and handle legal affairs. Given the lack of progress in the coronavirus pandemic, we can't make any definitive meeting plans. Ying Yue is disappointed. I feel the same.

When the situation improves, I'll go to Providence. I'll take the Chinese beauty cruising on my yacht. She interrupts me with flirting messages and steamy photos. The Shibari one is my favorite. When I'm with my young Asian lovers, I make use of the ropes.

Naughty Bim provides me regular deliveries and services. During her visits, she orgasms. I'm more to her than just a piggy bank. We meet each other's needs. Bim prefers me to masturbation because she doesn't get paid at home. Our deal works. She enjoys my company, and the spice I add to her life. Trapped in my apartment, I welcome physical contact.

Sweet Miss Nguyen and I grow closer. We share personal things, and our sex life is a laboratory. She wants to experiment. We order sex toys from Amazon. I pray their database never gets hacked. Cam-Tu gives herself to me completely because she fears losing me to Bim.

Cam-Tu's companionship improves my life one hundredfold. She gives me stability. She's lonely. I eliminate her loneliness. Being in a foreign country, during a pandemic, isn't easy. I give her security. I've started giving her some financial support too. She's living well because of my generosity. I'm considering buying her a new car.

My head hasn't been screwed on right during this world-wide disaster. If Cam-Tu wasn't there for me, I might have succumbed to depression. She always cheers me up, through her optimism and cute smile. Her people have been through far worse. Without Cam-Tu, I wouldn't be writing. I'm indebted to her.

The coronavirus prevents gatherings and normal social contact. I'm part of a colossal screw up. My loving parents are dead. I blame COVID-19 for turning me into a hermit, and damaging my psyche. I can't say if I'll recover. I mean ever. I stare out the window at the Naval Academy's Chapel. I lose track of time.

CHAPTER 34

THE EXQUISITE Buriram girl and the Navy SEAL mingled their beautiful bodies. After uncountable orgasms, Star surprised Tom by wanting to use the pool. When she put on her floss bikini, it appeared tan lines were no longer a concern. He offered to carry the bronze Thai goddess to the pool, if she agreed to wear her clear-plastic boots. She complied. His foot fetish made her weightless.

At the pool, Tom impressed his girlfriend with incredible breath-holding ability.

"You frog man ka. Same Froggy ka."

"Yeah."

"Me li-eh Froggy."

Since their initial meeting, Star's English improved, as did her confidence.

"Come here, Froggy. You know dowry?"

"Dowry? I've heard of it. Isn't it a chest or gift an engaged man gives to …"

"Mai kow jai ka. Me explain you. Dowry money you give family. In Thai, man give dowry woman him marry. Kow jai mai naka?"

"Oh, I see. Yes, that's …"

"When man marry Thai, him give money family Thai girl ka. Kow jai mai naka?"

"Okay, I …"

"That money go family. They raise Thai girl ka. Kow jai mai naka?"

"I see. It's payback, for raising a Thai daughter. The family gets money from the future husband?"

"Ka."

Star nodded. She smiled. Tom smiled. She intended to marry him. Her bringing up the dowry issue excited him. He understood the concept, but he didn't know the amount. For a poor Thai family in Issarn, he guessed a few thousand dollars. Because of Star's beauty, the family decided years ago that 3,999,999 baht (130,000 US dollars) was the right amount. Nine is a lucky number for Thai people. Tom loved her. He didn't intend to lose her over money.

The American had learned things are done differently in Thailand. Adapting the Thai philosophy, he decided to worry about the dowry, when the time came. He wouldn't sacrifice now for the future. Although neither Star nor her family ever saved any money, they hoped her rich American boyfriend did.

After another epic bedroom session and shower, Tom helped Star load the Camry. This time she gathered all her belongings. After the dowry chat, he knew she wanted to get married. He felt happy. As she was about to depart, Star leaned out and planted a possessive kiss on Tom's mouth.

"You kiss me anytime, Doc."

"You're so sweet and sexy, Star."

"Bpak wan. Korp khun naka."

"I'll miss you."

"Ka."

Star knows when to reassure a man. Whenever she kissed Tom under her own initiative, his love blossomed. He kissed her flush lips again. She blushed. As the Navy SEAL waved, his lover sped away down the soi. Something troubled the bronze Thai goddess.

When Tom returned to his apartment, he found a text from Gai: Need sex you. Need see blue eye ka. Sex long time. 555. He recognized Gai's use of '555' to represent 'haa, haa, haa.' He laughed. The little Thai masseuse had fallen in love with the handsome American. Gai figured she was pregnant. If she was, she wanted his support. She wanted to get married.

Tom missed calls from the ladyboys—one from Wan and two from Bpee. He missed seeing Bpee.

He kept his distance though, because of unanswered questions about his own nature. Wan is fun, but Tom missed Pan. She pushed the right buttons. Tom didn't return Wan's calls. She felt disappointed. If things didn't work with Star, Pan could fill her shoes.

Pan wanted a serious relationship with her American co-worker. He is handsome, rich, and a great lover. She liked his personality. They got along well both in and out of bed. She never met a man like him, and she feared never meeting another. Many farangs whom she met in Thailand were poor. They came to Thailand because of its low cost, for partying, or to meet bargirls. Many of them were gay. Despite working in a bar, Pan rarely went with customers. Although a generous and kind man, her Japanese boyfriend is too old for her to marry.

CHAPTER 35

Growing up, Kimberly Diamond was Tom's first true love. He carried her books from school, and they pretended to be married. She's the first girl whom Tom kissed. Before he joined the Navy SEALs, they came close to getting engaged. However, due to his dangerous missions, he'd postponed proposing to Kimberly.

Tom didn't want her to become a widow. They'd discussed marriage often. Once the Navy SEAL saw intense action, Kimberly noticed a change in his personality. Distance kept them apart, and gradually, their many-year relationship simmered. They never officially broke up, but Kimberly never cared for anyone else. Tom decided to call her.

"Hello, Kim."

"Tom? Tommie, is that you?"

"Yes."

"It's been so long. You sound so far away."

"Yeah, it's me Kimmy."

"Where are you, Tommie?"

"Thailand. A place called Chiang Mai."

"Geez, how long has it been?"

"Much too long. Sorry, I've been one poor correspondent. But, it doesn't mean you weren't on my mind. You were always on my mind. You were always on my mind, Kimmy."

"Oh, Tommie. I know. All your secret missions … stuff for the country. Top-secret stuff."

Kimberly knew Tom had left the agency. Rumors circulated that he'd been kicked out. She planned to avoid the topic.

"You seeing anyone?"

"Well yeah, Kimmy. That's actually what I'm calling about."

"Tommie, tell me."

"She's a real looker, Kim. Bronze skin like glittery body paint. Great figure. Her name's Star. A young Thai woman. Sweet. Kinky girl."

"Tommie, tell me more. What's her background? Family situation?"

"She's from northeast Thailand. A place called Buriram, in Issarn. They have a pro soccer team there. Probably comes from a poor family. I don't know if she has brothers or sisters. We never talked about her parents. In Issarn, there are different customs. I mean different from other parts of Thailand, not only the US. They love Americans."

"I think that started in the Vietnam War: 'Me love you long time.' "

"Miss Diamond!"

"Does she know you're, were with the SEALs? Does she know your history?"

Kimberly intentionally omitted the word 'violent.'

"No … nope. But, those things don't matter. If I settle here, that stuff will never come up again."

"Yeah, Tommie, I hope not."

The conversation continued with few pauses. Kimberly sounded supportive. She was doing well. She wasn't seeing anyone. After a long catch-up session, Tom eventually told Kimberly the real purpose of his call.

"Kim, I think I'm going to propose to her."

Kim's heart sank.

"Wow, Tommie! Isn't that sudden? Are you sure she's the right girl?"

"Kim, I'm not sure of anything anymore. It feels right. I'm thinking … I'm thinking maybe, I'll give it a try."

"You've been away a long time, Tommie. You've changed. I always knew you weren't someone to back down from anything. You always wanted the best, and went for it. 'One speed only, full throttle,' you used to say. Remember? And, if she means that much to you, well, go for it."

"Hearing that means a lot, Kim. Thanks."

"Hey, listen. My battery's about to die. Don't be such a stranger. Let me know how it goes, okay? I want the final verdict."

"Thanks, Kim."

"Remember, you always have me back home. Love you, Tommie. Love you very, very much."

"Thanks, Kim. Love you too."

"Good-bye."

"Good-bye."

Kimberly burst into tears. Tom felt uneasy with her sadness. She wanted to come to Thailand. He decided not to invite her, at least not until after the wedding. Kimmy means a lot to him. Being the tender-hearted person she is, she supported his decision. She didn't want to make Tom second guess himself. She continues to dream.

Tom planned to propose to Star. He would need to purchase an engagement ring. He would check his finances concerning the dowry. The Navy SEAL felt confident.

CHAPTER 36

A FLURRY OF MESSAGES arrived from Daniels. The cyber war with China heated up. A group of hackers in Kunming were plotting cyberattacks on the United States. Tom continued monitoring the Chinese on a low-bandwidth connection to avoid detection. The process was tedious. Dr. Jones wanted him to review the information coming out of Ugly Gorilla's group as well. A set of trained eyes might pick up something the AI programs missed.

The intelligence already gathered had helped them thwart a denial of service attack on the Federal Employees Retirement System. They also blocked an attempt the PLA had made to hack the TWSE. The mainland wasn't happy with Taiwan. Although data being collected in another stream were inconclusive, they suggested that the Chinese were experimenting with a new biological weapon at one of their labs in Wuhan. They were using bats in their research. Several scientists had died mysteriously.

Oh, my God. I wonder if it's the coronavirus. I'm glad the team is running surveillance. We need people like Tom and Cody keeping a watchful eye. I wonder if I should contact the government.

The agency monitored calls and Internet traffic from the Chinese government's Wuhan lab. Jones's team were slowly piecing together a complex puzzle. Their analysis led to the identification of a social network that included top communist-party officials, research scientists, medical doctors, and others in the PLA who had been involved in biological warfare in the past. Dr. Jones wanted his team to keep a close eye on the emerging situation.

Through stolen documents, Jones's group had learned that Chinese-government employees are trained in information-technology security procedures, restricting them from opening WORD email attachments. The team found no such requirements regarding PDF files. Some party members probably felt secure in opening a PDF-file attachment, especially if the file appeared to come from inside their network from a trusted source.

Tom continued his work on the development of a zero-day exploit for PDF files. He created a document using the Book Antiqua font and found that when certain hidden-character sequences are embedded in the right file, he could cause a buffer overflow. He could take control of a PDF viewer by resetting the code's instruction pointer to begin executing a series of implanted system commands.

Once his software gained control, he could force the system to execute his embedded malware in its entirety.

A spear-fishing attack originating from a valid email address in Shanghai, and directed to key people in Kunming and Wuhan, could open up digital beach heads, providing critical information about China's biological weapons program.

I slap my thigh.

Based on email content and recipient patterns that they'd been analyzing, Tom selected an account to spoof. He chose a prominent Shanghai official, Dr. Hong Dong, who frequently sent out English-language memos as PDF attachments. Tom's team carefully cloned one of Dong's messages.

From Dr. Dong's account, the Navy SEAL sent the fake message to the usual recipients. The message contained Tom's buffer-overflow malware, as a PDF attachment. For the attack to be successful, he only needed one of Dong's associates to take the bait. They hoped for takers in both Kunming and Wuhan. For the moment, Dr. Jones put all his eggs in one basket, as he couldn't divulge the information already gathered about Wuhan, or its covert source.

If Tom made another major breakthrough, or clear-cut facts damning the Chinese for violating the Chemical Weapons Convention became available, Dr. Jones and his superior could take things to the Director of the NSA and the President. At that juncture, Cody would need to come clean about his rogue operations in Southeast Asia. Only if a true catastrophe could be prevented would he bring his team out in the open, and discuss the Thailand operations. He needed his team to succeed.

The entire world needs them to succeed.

***

Daniels assembled Pan, Wan, Manow, Mae, and Uan, as a squad to eliminate a key, Chinese-female agent. As an experienced killer, Tom would be the one to execute her. When he learned that the agent was non-other than Ugly Gorilla's wife, Ah Kum, he asked Daniels for confirmation. When the confirmation came back, Tom experienced a sinking feeling. In a bizarre twist, unknown to Ugly Gorilla himself, his wife worked for the PLA too.

Ironically, the information streamed back, from the laptop that Ah Kum had stolen, condemned her to death. She was the Chinese agent referred to in Dr. Jones's handwritten note to Tom back at Fort Meade. They learned that Ah Kum would be returning to Chiang Mai in another month without Ugly Gorilla, as the Thais preferred working with her to her husband. Tom would be meeting with Ah Kum one final time.

It seems Tom is getting well-deserved redemption. I decide to take a break and open an email from the Dean. His cordial messages keep me in the loop at the Naval Academy.

Many activities are postponed or delayed, but his workload increases. He mentioned the Navy captain who'd been fired from the USS Theodore Roosevelt. A number of Academy graduates contracted the coronavirus in their deployments. Although the Navy is receiving not-so-favorable press, the Dean assured me things will be back to normal by the time my leave ends.

I've made a dent in my liquor cabinet. Cam-Tu and I usually share a drink or two. Bim will be coming over this afternoon. Whenever I get a buildup of empties, I ask her to recycle them for me. Bim doesn't seem to fear going outside. At least, she doesn't complain. Perhaps she lived through the SARs epidemic in Asia. She's comfortable in a mask. I never probe into her personal affairs. I only know what she offers.

I poke around the folders on the laptop. I learn the novels are in a different order than I thought. I move to the file Part30Star. I'm eager to wrap up my work. There are only a few parts left to edit. I want to see how Tom's proposal goes. Good luck with that, ole boy. She's a real looker—a bronze Thai goddess.

CHAPTER 37

THE BRONZE THAI goddess gave her American boyfriend directions to her penthouse. Tom asked for clarifications, so as not to expose his familiarity. As he pocketed the engagement ring, he exhaled forcefully. The commitment to his dream Thai girl is a huge step. Marriage meant changes to his care-free lifestyle. Star was worth it.

Tom waited outside. His tuk-tuk driver dropped him in front of Star's apartment on Huay Kaew Road. He walked past the sleeping security guard. Tom was amazed the guard slept through the blaring soap opera. On the screen, he caught a glimpse of a young Thai girl, and what appeared to be a crying suitor. The Navy SEAL kept his head down, while moving to the elevator.

Tom rang Star's bell. She answered in a skin-tight, full-body catsuit. He could see no flesh, except her round eyes and voluptuous lips. Silver buckles lined the arms and legs of the suit. The platform heels raised the stunning girl to eye level. Black latex gloves covered her hands. Her hair snaked out a hole in the glossy suit.

"A Siamese cat of a girl. You're amazing! I love it. You're the sexiest woman alive!"

"Korp khun ka. Meow. Meow. He, he, he."

The suit modified the kinky-girl's voice. She made scratching motions.

"I love red lipstick. Your mouth in that hood—whoa!"

"Meow."

The perverted seductress led Tom toward the bedroom. On the way through the kitchen, he noticed that the knives and meat cleaver hadn't moved. He recognized things that he'd bought. Other than the photo of Star with the pudgy businessman, everything else appeared the same. She'd struggled to get into the catsuit. When they entered the bedroom, she was overheating.

The bronze Thai goddess needed an orgasm. Donning the tight latex suit aroused her, as did prancing around self-voyeuristically, checking her look in the mirror. Tom's proposal needed to wait. With her gloves, she couldn't try on the ring. He didn't want her removing anything.

Tom desired the Thai pussy. The meowing, black feline stripped him. She dropped to her knees. Star spit. The saliva-lubricated gloves got him started. In the mirror, Tom gawked at her bobbing head. The stretchy suit fit more snuggly than her bronze skin. Her ponytail bounced around in a serpentine manner. Her aura unleashed an apocalyptic storm of desire within him.

"I'm burning … I'm burning for you."

"Catsuit have small hole."

"Will I fit?"

"Ka. Me love you long time," Star imitated a bargirl's voice.

While moaning and meowing, Star slithered on the silky sheets, making suggestive gestures. Her provocative movements incited reckless behavior. Tom's creative juices flowed, and he decided to mount the sexy feline in a new position. He kneeled in front of his panther. Before the teasing girl realized it, he'd forced her heels behind her ears.

The slit in the catsuit's opening aligned perfectly. With the bronze Thai goddess's heels pinned, Tom entered. Her knees pressed outward. The folding position shifted her organs forward. He exerted himself. Her ebullient entrance expanded. She reached behind the backs of her knees. She pulled. The narrow opening in the catsuit widened.

Star told him to go harder. Tom obeyed. Although his dripping sweat ran off, she boiled in hers. The heat generated from being encased in the non-breathable fabric powered her debauched actions. Her kinky nature reaffirmed his plan to propose marriage.

"Me close again ka. Reo, reo."

CHAPTER 38

L UKTUNG MUSIC blared from Star's mobile. "Kor-toht ka. Minute ka."

The abysmal timing angered Tom. He was seconds from climaxing. He reluctantly slowed. She reached for the phone. He listened. Shocked, he stared and paused. Tom prayed the caller wasn't her other lover. He thought that situation had been resolved. Doubt crept in regarding his marriage proposal.

"My sister ka. Keep going, keep riding me … Sa waa dii ka."

Tom felt relieved. He continued, as requested.

"You busy? Sound busy ka?"

"No, me with Doc. Me not hear wery good. Catsuit cover ear. He, he, he."

"Catsuit? I call you back."

"No, you talk him ka. She talk you, Doc."

"Now?"

"Ka. Keep going. Hard."

After giving him the mobile, Star returned her hands to the backs of her knees. She tugged.

"Hi. Uh, I'm Doc."

"Ha-low, I twin Star. Me name Dee ka."

"Dee?"

"She Dee. She twin Star."

"Twin sister?"

"Ka."

Tom was confused.

"Twin?"

"Ka."

Tom couldn't believe it.

"Does 'dee' mean good?"

"Ka. Dee mean good ka. But, I bad. He, he, he."

"You look like Star?"

"She twin me."

"Wow!"

Tom blew out a puff of air. While he conversed with Dee, Star rocked her curled body and pressed into him. Her motions sent him on a wild ride. A froth forming at the catsuit's slit caused a magnificent tingling, as though someone held a recently opened bottle of champagne there.

Dee's luscious voice resonated sexily. Talking to her, while inside Star, thrilled Tom fantastically. He maintained balance, while gripping the phone. The Navy SEAL synchronized his hip movements with Star's thrusting.

"Dee li-eh sex too much. Li-eh me ka," Star said.

"Star say you big size ka. Thin' of me," Dee requested.

"I didn't know Star had a sister, never mind a twin."

"She have me. Dee ka. I want hear you."

Dee gave orders to Tom. She stripped and touched herself. She described what she was doing. She told him what to do to her twin. Throughout their lives, Star and Dee had competed against one another. They made each other jealous. Dee wanted to win this competition.

"I wish you were here, Dee."

"Me too. Three together. Boom-boom. Twin, same same ka."

"That would be amazing!"

Dee's steamy sounds, provocations, and instructions; combined with Star's moaning; and the revelation that she has a twin mixed Tom's chemicals to the point where he lost rationality. He thought Star was unique. Dee elevated the green-faced man's high and took control of his mind.

"I touchin' myself ka. When I thin' about you, I touchin' myself."

"Keep touching yourself. Keep talking. Tell me what you're doing."

Dee provided description. She moaned.

"I need you inside me. Neeaw mahk ka," Dee said.

"Star getting close ka."

"Me all wet ka. You want get inside me?"

"Yes, I would love that, Dee."

Tom wondered if he'd spoken out loud. Dee barked orders.

"Yeah, Dee that's good. What do you want me to do to her now?"

Dee gave instructions. Tom followed them.

"Me coming soon."

"I almost coming ka," Star moaned.

"We come together."

"Think Dee, you come inside she. Her jealous ka. Okay?" Dee requested.

"Yeah, I'm thinking of you, Dee."

"You want boom-boom with she ka?" Star asked.

"Yeah, baby. If she looks like you."

"She twin me ka."

"You want come in me?" Dee asked.

"Yeah, Dee."

"Come in me ka," Star said.

"Come in me," Dee demanded.

Tom started the countdown, "Haa, see, sahm …"

The three synchronized in an emotional and physical crescendo. The twins moaned and groaned. Tom grunted. They all exclaimed their powerful orgasms.

"Dee set sorng krang."

"Me come three time," Star lied.

"You're sexy, Dee."

"Dee go now. Hope see you soon ka."

"Good-bye, Dee."

"Tell Star bye ka. Bye-bye."

Even while Star's resentment built, she'd emboldened her American boyfriend's behavior, as it excited her wildly. When Tom had pretended to finish inside her twin sister, Star experienced a jealous feeling similar to the one at the Panviman Spa. She hated the little Thai masseuse who'd received her boyfriend's gift there. Now, Star felt anger toward Dee. Star's emotions seesawed, never in balance.

The bronze Thai goddess's endorphins and the yah-bah that she'd taken created a charged mixture in her blood, which acted as an aphrodisiac. Her anger, pain, and jealously added more chemicals. The blend produced an uncontrollable euphoria. Star encouraged Tom's forays to help her achieve this state. However, once she came down, she deeply regretted where his penis had gone, and where he wanted it to go.

A woman as rapacious and covetous as the bronze Thai goddess needs complete devotion. Although her negative emotions contributed to her best orgasms, the aftermath always left her feeling troubled. Star felt shattered and unattractive. She didn't realize that she'd brought these problems on herself.

Tom never picked up on Star's attitude shift. His deep infatuation with her meant that he loved her unconditionally. Small issues never mattered. He focused too much on the physical aspects of their relationship, and not enough on the psycho-logical side. Although she exhibited mental instabil-ity, due to his own problems, her internal struggles never bothered him.

CHAPTER 39

TOM FELT HAPPY the black Siamese cat had insisted on answering her phone. Their three-some went beyond his fantasies—a tag team of clones of the bronze Thai goddess. They're bad girls, which is good.

"You two are naughty."

"Dee wery sexy. Dee good girl. Me bad girl ka. Her more beautiful me ka."

"No, Star, you're the most beautiful woman in the whole wide world."

"Dee wery hot. Star no joke ka."

"I want to ask you to m … That's my phone. Moment."

"Ka."

The call originated from an unknown number. If Star hadn't answered her call, he wouldn't have answered his. As Tom reached, he remained inside the black Siamese goddess. Thoughts of the twins thrilled him. Star rocked.

"Excuse me, dear." Tom answered, "Hello."

"Ha-low. Mister, this Star husband. I know you have been seeing my wife. If you see her again, I kill you. I kill you. Kow jai mai?"

"What?"

"Farang man bad. Thai man good. I Star husband. I marry Star. I warn you, if you see her again, I kill you. Kow jai mai?"

Tom pushed harder and farther into Star.

"She's here now. Star, are you married? She never told me. Huh?"

Star realized it was her husband calling. Horrified, she was unable to respond. She froze. Her refusal to answer, the tears running down the catsuit, and her open mouth drove Tom crazy. He continued banging her, becoming spiteful, as he listened to the threats on his life.

"Star my wife. You no see Star again, or I kill you. Kow jai mai?"

Something deep inside the Navy SEAL snapped. He flashed back to a violent mission—one involving gross misconduct. He placed the phone next to Star's head. Her husband listened. In a rage, Tom turned her into a contortionist. In an untamed temper, the aggrieved man began a sadistic beating to liberate his indignation. In an eye-for-an-eye retaliation, he would right her wrong.

"You're married?"

With each punishing blow, no answer came from the panicking Siamese cat.

"You're married?"

"You hurt me ka."

"You're married?"

"Ow, ow. I hurt."

"When were you going to tell me?"

"Stop ka. I hurt. You hurt Star. Please ka."

"I'm going to come in you, Star."

"No stop. Please stop ... ow. Don't come inside me. My husband hear you. He hear us. Please ka. I beg you. He hear you come in me. You coming?"

"I can't believe you, bitch. I'm coming in you. I'm coming in you like all those other times, when you told me how much you loved me ... remember? I came in you many times. You wanted it."

"Me feel you coming inside ... noooo ... stop ka. You come inside?"

"Too late, bitch. I'm finished. I just dumped my giant American load in your married little Thai pussy. Hear that asshole?"

"You hurt me. You fuck me too hard. Look. You come dripping out ... You come in me too much. I sorry. Star wery sorry. Look ... I think I pregnant."

"You said you loved me forever. You remember your words, 'I will always love you'?"

Tom belligerently withdrew from the shamed Thai girl. Star had chewed a hole in the catsuit. As his juice ran down her thighs, she sobbed. A bloody spray had turned the bed sheet into a Jackson Pollock painting. Tom shook his head. He'd given her that bedding.

Tom picked up the phone. He declared slowly, loudly, and clearly, "I just filled your wife with my hot American come. She smiled, enjoyed me screwing her, and came repeatedly. Kow jai mai? Goodbye."

While the humiliated husband continued talking, Tom hung up. The furious Thai man was mortified. His face turned red. Tom resisted slapping Star's face. He pushed her away.

"You do bad thin'. Him big Thai man. Business man ka."

"I do bad thing? Are you fucking married?"

"Ka."

"When were you going to tell me?"

"Star love you, but me already marry. Me need marry for family. Me need money. Lots of money. Me love money ka. Me too young."

"We went everywhere in public—shopping, to restaurants, bars ... I bought you all those things. Oh, Christ."

"I sorry. Star in trouble ka. Me wery sorry you."

"Things were going great. We had such a good time. I loved you ... See. I was going to give you this today. I can't support you anymore. I need time to think."

"Me no want lose you. Star wery big problem ka."

"We talked about a dowry ... amazing Thailand. I guess I should have ..."

"Me wery sorry ka."

Sitting with her arms folded, bleeding, and suffocating from the pressure of the catsuit, the shamed Thai girl no longer felt like a sexy dominatrix, but rather a humiliated fool.

Tom's proposal vaporized with her husband's call. He couldn't fathom that his bronze Thai goddess was married already. He couldn't accept that fact. The responsibility of telling him that she's married fell on Star, but she never had said anything. She never wore a wedding ring.

Star put Tom's life in grave danger by parading him around so many public venues. The couple could have been seen by her husband's friends, or even worse, by him. Her adulterous behavior put Tom's life in jeopardy.

The Navy SEAL was flabbergasted that a married woman had held his hand in public. And, he only just learned his lover had a twin sister. If they'd gotten married, he could see now that there would have been many other surprises too—mostly disappointing ones.

You're damn right there would have been, ole boy. I'm glad you found out that she's married before you gave her a dowry. You would have lost a lot of money. The nerve of that Issarn girl is mind boggling.

I hope Tom survives this disaster. I believe he will. He's a Navy SEAL.

***

Ejaculating inside the bronze Thai goddess one final time, as her despondent husband listened and threatened, provided Tom retribution and relief, but enraged her husband. Star's husband wanted vengeance and planned to kill the American. She wanted her husband's financial support, more material possessions, and his forgiveness. Tom no longer knew what he wanted.

CHAPTER 40

IN THE PAST, STAR witnessed how easily her Issarn girlfriends used subterfuge and manipulated farang men. The bronze Thai goddess learned her lessons well. She'd controlled her American boyfriend easily through sex and sweet talk. Star's affair incited her husband's jealously and provided the leverage that she needed to negotiate a higher monthly allowance, in return for her loyalty.

Star loathed her husband, and she hated his name too—Anuman "John" Banakraptommanatorn. However, John's money determined her quality of life and level of self-esteem. Using her physical gifts, she manipulated her husband and others. Men always forgave her misdeeds and digressions. Due to cultural differences, manipulating Thai men requires a different skill set than for farangs. She'd mastered both.

Star's extraordinary beauty gives her an edge over men. They always give her what she wants. Despite her furnished penthouse, new car, extensive wardrobe, silk bedding, modern china and cutlery sets, shoe collection, fetish clothing, sex toys, iPhone, laptop, cosmetics, and substantial monthly allowance, Star craved more. Her ambition reaches far beyond her upbringing in a two-room, bamboo hut in a small village in Buriram.

John originally owned a couple of 7-11s in Buriram. The day that the twinkling beauty walked into one of them, altered his life forever. Regardless of what it cost him, he needed to marry the stunning Issarn girl. The massive dowry required by the girl's poor Issarn family almost ruined John, and sent him spiraling into debt. To finance the Buriram beauty and her family, he became involved in crime.

The risky nature of John's illegal dealings never troubled him. When Star is involved, ethics, the law, and dangers matter little. The regular and sizeable deposits into his bank account were well worth the associated risks. He never felt like he had much choice. Once he saw the bronze Thai goddess, her spell mesmerized him. Reason abandoned him.

John's requirement for obtaining vast sums of money stemmed from Star's expensive shopping habits and material needs. Little of his support actually went to her family in Buriram. They still lived in the hut. Star had kept most of the wedding dowry for herself. She controlled her family too.

Prior to Star's entrance into John's life, he lived comfortably on the income from his convenience stores. For his entire life though, John felt physically inadequate, due to his small penis. Marrying a woman whom everyone felt envious of gave him great pride and boosted his confidence. As John's ego grew, in his own mind, so did his manhood.

John never met Star's physical needs, but as her sugar daddy, he owned her. To keep her salary flowing, she needed to grant his wishes. Bewitched by her beauty, John obsessed about possessing her. When they were apart, he worried what his wife was doing. John knows he can't trust an Issarn girl. The American would pay for John's carelessness.

John's chicanery expanded along with Star's aspirations. In a materialistic culture, where appearances matter more than truth, they became entangled in a web of deceit, as they attempted to climb higher in Thai society. The pair fueled one another's goals and desires; they lost touch with reality, and any sense of propriety.

***

Star depended on and loved John's money. His upcoming deal would provide him sufficient funds to satisfy his wife's demands for the immediate future. He never looks too much beyond the present. He can't afford to. When John agreed to increase Star's allowance, she felt in control again. She felt valued and important.

John believed that in killing Star's American boyfriend, he could win back his wife's loyalty. His demonstration of extreme force would prevent Star from ever threatening to leave him. He felt an urgent need to save face. The American stepped in his way; the American slept with his wife; the American taunted him; the American needed to die.

John never considered that he couldn't satisfy Star in bed, that her licentious behavior might have been the root of his problems with her, or that his wife might have done something wrong. To all Thai men, Star is infallible. With her presence alone, a woman as beautiful as the bronze Thai goddess increases the status of a man. To self-validate and prove their success, Thai businessmen need to have pretty women hanging off their arms. John was a Thai businessman.

John hates farangs because they always get the pick of the litter. When his first Thai girlfriend left him for a handsome farang, he was only 15. He experienced the same heartbreak at ages 18, 24, 28, 33, and 39, and his hatred for farangs grew. Now, the familiar pattern repeated itself. Although Star never wore a wedding ring, John's ego is so big that he believes everyone should know she belongs to him, even if no one ever tells them. Her affair sentenced the Navy SEAL to death.

***

Over the phone, Star and her husband coordinated a plan of action. She would lure her American lover to her penthouse. From there, John and his henchmen would take care of things. She knew they intended to kill the American. The callous girl thought only of herself. She always viewed him as an ATM, and there were other ATMs available.

Star's deserted penthouse floor lacked any security. John and his two bodyguards planned to take the American by surprise. While Star went out on an errand, they would murder her lover in her room. Although John wanted Star to know that he killed her American boyfriend, he didn't want Star there seeing his brutality. John looked forward to disfiguring the American's face, burning his hands, pulling out his teeth, and disposing of his body in the murky Ping River. If the body ever were found, it wouldn't be identifiable.

Their jointly plotted, cruel scheme, devoid of any emotional reaction from her, proved Star's loyalty to John, and that she never had possessed sincere feelings for the American. Her ruthless nature, driven by greed, put Tom in grave danger. The murder of Star's lover would satisfy John's need for revenge, against the many farangs who'd wronged him.

Although Star strongly preferred her blue-eyed American hunk in bed, John's reliable payments won her allegiance. She would miss her fantastic orgasms, but she didn't love the American. She loved his body, and the feeling of being seen with a handsome farang man. Because of her vanity, Star could replace him with a mirror, toys, and drugs. His disappearance wouldn't cause her any remorse. She wanted to save herself. Star's true love is money. Without requiring sexual favors, money grants one's wishes. Money changes everything.

Star's full cooperation and collaboration against the American would wipe her slate clean, win back John's trust, and earn his forgiveness. She promised to be faithful. She agreed to wear her wedding ring. She consented to avoid farangs. She went along with all John's demands.

John boosted Star's allowance from 50,000 to 75,000 baht per month. For her birthday, he would give her a 100,000-baht bonus. He would continue to pay for her penthouse, car insurance, beauty needs, and other sundry bills. She could still use the beauty salon and take money from its cash register, whenever she felt like it. The arrangement suited them.

Under their deal's terms, Star could maintain her lavish lifestyle. John planned to come visit and show her off at least a few days per month. Because he worked in Bangkok, she still would retain a great deal of freedom. She wouldn't have to spend too much time with a husband whom she disliked.

If a more lucrative opportunity came along, Star would figure out how to escape from her husband and take advantage of it. She focused on the present. Once the American disappeared, John didn't anticipate any more problems with his wife. His ego would be restored. They would be able to continue, as a happily married couple.

CHAPTER 41

I STARE OUT THE window at the Naval Academy's Chapel. I mumble, "Tom, you're not the first American, and you won't be the last, to be duped by an Issarn girl. Star betrayed you. Stay on your toes."

My effort to bring the story to the Nobel level of writing has made me weary. My drinking has contributed. I don't want to see Tom die. I hope Star will have a change of heart and save him. She must realize how much he loves her.

With a glass in hand, I tip my head back and gravity does its thing. I grab the table's edge. I open the file Part35Star.

Tom finally realized and admitted that the bronze Thai goddess used him as a pawn in a game against her husband. Using Maker's Mark, he tried to drown his sorrows. He failed. He became sick.

I'm here with you, ole boy.

Tom reached a highpoint at the Panviman Resort. While sitting at Baan Ketawa, he sank to a troubling low. The Thai-wife objective was out of reach. Daniels's messages indicated that something big was brewing. Getting involved in a mission would help him snap out of his depression. It would focus him. Tom wanted to call Kimberly Diamond, but she was asleep.

***

Tom received an image from Daniels of the Thai spy guilty of selling secrets to the Chinese. The man looked familiar. When Tom scanned through the photos in his phone, he located the guy. The man in Daniels's photo is Star's husband—a wealthy Thai businessman named Anuman Banakraptom-manatorn. Dressed in the same suit, as in the picture that Tom had snapped in Star's apartment, there could be no mistaking the short, fat man.

Tom's search on his mobile forced him to scan through many images of the bronze Thai goddess. With his incomparably beautiful Thai wife lost forever, the meanings associated with those photos morphed into hurtful memories, sparking negative emotions. He closed the phone. He shook his head in disgust. On the verge of eternal happiness, he now walked a tightrope. It was hard not to fall.

Daniels wanted Tom to eliminate the Thai traitor, Mr. Banakraptommanatorn, as soon as possible. Their intelligence indicated an impending sale of top-secret data. The transfer might happen any day. Daniels didn't possess the details yet. His team was working on it.

Following the trail of deposits into Banakrap-tommanatorn's bank account, they realized that he normally received a retainer, and two days later, a second, far-larger payment. Intelligence suggested the second amount came in, after his job was complete. The record of a recent deposit meant Tom and his team needed to act.

***

Pan and Wan visited Tom at Baan Ketawa to discuss their upcoming hit. Although sexual innuendos flew around, business took precedence. Using the tap on Star's mobile, Pan determined Mr. Banakrap-tommanatorn planned to arrive at Star's apartment with his two bodyguards at 7:30 PM. Star planned to invite Doc to come over at 7:00 PM. The three men planned to kill the Navy SEAL in Star's apartment. Pan, Wan, and Tom formulated a plan to keep him alive and eliminate their target.

Tom knew Daniels possessed a far-reaching network and began to question whether the original meeting with Star hadn't been orchestrated. He wondered about Pan's level of involvement, and how much she knew about his relationship with Star. The same questions applied to Wan. The coincidence of the spy whom he needed to eliminate being Star's husband proved too much for the Navy SEAL to accept at face value. When he left Dr.

Jones's office back at Fort Meade on that fateful day, Tom's private life ended.

Pan needed to clear their plan with Daniels. Once given the go ahead, she would share the details with Manow and Uan, and explain their roles. If the operation succeeded, it would be a huge win for the team and the agency. It would provide additional validation of Dr. Jones's decision to retain Tom and send him to Thailand.

To celebrate their victory, Tom, Pan, and Wan planned to get drunk and have a ménage à trois. He cautioned that they were getting ahead of themselves. Their full attention needed to be on the mission—a failure meant his death. No one seemed as concerned about that outcome, as he did.

A while after Pan and Wan departed, Star phoned. As anticipated, she invited him over at 7:00 PM, with the idea of patching up their relationship. She lied easily. Tom played along. She promised him that she would leave her husband. Without the contrary information from Pan's phone tapping, he would have believed Star. She was convincing.

The bronze Thai goddess enticed Tom by telling him that her twin sister, Dee, would be there. Star knew his hopes for twins would occupy his mind. Tom feigned an overwhelming interest in making things right. He made Star jealous by expressing his desire for Dee. In a warped way, his desire for her twin increased her desire for him.

Tom told the conniving girl that he would bring her engagement ring. Star wanted the ring, and she planned to get it. She could make a lot of money by pawning a large diamond. When Pan learned about the ring, she wanted it too. Tom intended to bring the ring to Star's penthouse, so as not to arouse her suspicions.

The conversation between Star and Tom made Pan jealous. Something about Star troubled Pan. If they accomplished their mission, she didn't want Star around. Manow and Uan would see to that aspect of the plan. Pan prayed things worked out, and that no one on their team got hurt, especially not the man whom she loved.

With Tom's emotions running amok from Star's betrayal, he wouldn't be at his best. The idea that the woman whom he planned to marry set him up to be murdered was incomprehensible. He couldn't wrap his head around her cold-blooded nature. Chiang Mai threw him a wicked curve ball. Tom struck out with Star, and he didn't want to lose the final inning to her husband.

The green-faced man simply couldn't accept the fact that Star is a married woman. Her lie crushed his psyche. In this moment of weakness, Tom needed to be strong, but he was vulnerable. He began to comprehend the power of Star's magical spell. If he fell into the bronze Thai goddess's trap again, this one would be his final mission.

Chapter 42

WAN AND PAN arrived together and parked on a soi near Star's building. Manow and Uan pulled up separately on their motorcycles. A tuk-tuk dropped Tom on the side of Huay Kaew Road, a couple blocks away from Star's apartment. Pan watched the handsome American walk toward her. On cue, she jammed the security cameras.

The security guard, captivated by a Thai soap opera, missed Tom and Pan, as they strode past. Wan lingered. She planned to follow the three thugs to the penthouse. She might be able to warn Tom. If any of the Thai men got out of the room, Wan and Pan would deal with them. The ladyboy prayed for Tom's success. Pan called on Buddha to watch over him.

Tom rang Star's bell at 7:00 PM. The kinky girl answered, dressed to kill, and planted a wet French kiss on his mouth. He accepted the bronze Thai goddess's tongue. The convincing kiss excited Tom.

The internal stress, which they each felt, added to their arousals.

After Star's profuse apology and pleading for forgiveness, they moved to the bedroom. Her incriminating photo was hidden. Tom wanted to get inside the bronze Thai goddess one final time. As things began to get hot and heavy, her mobile rang—the call came in on schedule. Tom recognized the ring tone.

"Ha-low," Star answered. "Dee ka. Moment ka."

"Sure."

Star spoke to Dee in the Issarn language. He waited. After the call ended, Star translated the gist of the conversation to the American.

"Dee arrive Chiang Mai ka. She wait airport. Me pick she up. Her not know you here ka. We surprise her. He, he, he. You okay ka?"

"While you pick up Dee, I wait here?"

"Ka."

"Okay, dear. Hurry back. I always dreamed of having twins."

Tom smiled convincingly. Star nodded.

"Star came back soon. Me have Dee ka. Khun chorp mahk ka. Two lady same look. Two lady same time. Twin ka."

Star laid it on thick. She described what they planned to do with him. He imagined crazy positions.

"Sounds fantastic. I'll be waiting."

"Ka. Good-bye, Doc."

"Bye, Star."

When the deceitful girl departed, without a final kiss, Tom's heart broke. In The Land of Smiles, he dated his fantasy girl. He came close to a happy ending. Just one moment away from proposing marriage, he learned his dream girl was married. In that devastating revelation, Tom's future-wife plans exploded. They were over now. He came close to marrying the wrong Thai woman.

"You're lucky, ole boy. Many farangs do marry the wrong Thai woman."

What hurt Tom the most is that Star never belonged to him. She never loved him. When they met, she was married. She used him for leverage and financial gain. Daniels and Jones used him. They used others too. Tom's anger ignited his need for revenge against Star's husband. The green-faced man clinched his fists. He let out a series of expletives.

Tom received a text from Pan that Star had departed. Uan followed her by motorcycle. Tom expected another text shortly, warning him about Star's husband's arrival. Although the traitor possessed a key to the penthouse, Star intentionally had left the front door unlocked. Tom locked it. This maneuver would buy him a few more seconds. He needed to move fast.

Tom raced into the living room and turned on the TV. He increased the volume of the Thai soap opera. On the way back through the kitchen, he grabbed the meat cleaver and whetstone from Star's set of knives. He began sharpening the cleaver, as he moved behind the front door. From that vantage point, he couldn't see into the living room, but he could hear the TV clearly.

Tom hid behind the front-door's entrance. When the warning message came from Wan, he silenced his phone. His urgency with the whetstone increased. Tom ran a finger over the meat-cleaver's edge. It was sharp. He set the whetstone down. He listened for the arrival of Star's husband and his cronies.

Wan hid one floor below the penthouse, waiting for her opportunity to move higher. While staying out of sight, Pan moved farther into the complex. Manow stood by ready for a call. As the Thai businessman exited the lift, his hatred for farangs erupted. John wanted revenge against the American for having sex with his wife. He would derive extreme pleasure from carving up the farang's face.

At the front door, Tom listened as the men who came to kill him removed their shoes. They could hear the TV. John knew the TV is in the living room. He spoke to his hitmen. The door knob turned. Although he'd told Star to leave the door unlocked, he assumed his gorgeous wife had forgotten. While reaching in his pocket, he shook his head.

Tom heard a key entering the lock and the men speaking softly in the Issarn language. His palms sweat. The Navy SEAL stared at the slow-turning doorknob. He glanced at the razor-sharp meat cleaver. As the door opened, the green-faced man waited to pounce. Thrust onto the battlefield by his married Thai girlfriend, his adrenaline surged.

Sweat dripped off Tom's forehead. An armed Thai hitman tiptoed in the direction of the noisy TV, followed closely by Star's stocky husband. They stared straight ahead, moving methodically. As the third man began to close the door, Tom saw a long suppressor on the hitman's gun. The Navy SEAL raised the meat cleaver up high and tightened his grip.

The last man to enter realized that his boss had made a horrible mistake. Before the shocked hitman could shout a warning, the Navy SEAL grabbed the hitman's wrist and swung the meat cleaver with precision. When the hitman's hand severed just above Tom's grip, blood sprayed. The thug aimed his wrist and attempted to pull the trigger, but failed. In denial about his amputation, the man stared at his stump, spraying blood on his face. His gun had changed hands. The Navy SEAL kicked the door shut.

The leading hitman turned. The green-faced man moved forward steadily. Using the amputee's detached finger, the Navy SEAL pulled the trigger twice. The bullets exploded the first hitman's head, adding a Caravaggio-red splash to the Buddhist images on the wall. The faceless man dropped. Tom walked backward a few steps, and with a spinning-backfist maneuver, planted the meat cleaver in the one-handed hitman's temple. Before the big Thai man hit the floor, he died.

The swooshes, thwacks, pops, and thuds glued Star's unarmed and confused husband to the floor. The muscular, raging American induced panic in the hateful Thai man. The Navy SEAL returned the gun and hand to its owner. He tossed the bloody meat cleaver too. The green-faced man charged Star's husband.

In broken English, Star's husband begged for mercy. The American spun the fat Thai man around in a headlock. John's pleas came far too late.

"You, fuck!"

While choking Star's husband, the Navy SEAL lifted the heavy man off the ground.

"I have a very particular set of skills, acquired through years of training with the US Special Forces. Refined in deserts around the world. If you had let Star go, that would have been the end of it. I would not have killed you. Now, mine will be the last face you ever see, you dumb, greedy fuck."

The Thai man peed. His final thought was one of his beautiful wife—she'd left the door unlocked. In one of his maniacal rages, the Navy SEAL swung Star's husband back and forth, until the traitor became a dripping, lifeless, ragdoll pendulum. With the targets down, Tom washed his feet, hands, and face. He called a vigilant and worried Pan.

"They're dead. It's over. Come up. When you enter, watch the blood. Let the others know too. I made a mess."

"I'm so glad you're okay. Be right up."

Pan, Wan, and Manow entered. The grizzly scene shocked them, and they slowed. Wan threw up. Pan hugged Tom.

"Glad you're okay."

"Thanks. Watch out, there's liquid everywhere. Let's get to work," Tom said. "Have Uan bring Star back here."

"She didn't get far," Pan said.

"I figured. Manow, you have the drugs? "

"Krap."

"Plant the drugs. Continue as we mapped things out. Take plenty of photos. Once I'm out of here, you can restart the security cameras, Pan. Get the real police involved, after Star's taken care of."

Tom put the word 'real' in air quotes, which brought a smile to Manow's face. In Thailand, he and Uan are the real police.

"We know what to do. You get out of here, Doc. Amazing work."

Pan refrained from saying, "I love you."

"I'll contact Daniels. Before you leave, grab a few things out of her closet for us, Pan," Tom winked. "When you look in there, you'll know what I'm talking about. You ladies get out of here, before the real police show up. Ha, ha, ha. Good luck."

Tom departed. The others arranged the scene to look like a drug deal gone horribly wrong.

***

Uan led Star into the doctored scene. The destruction caused a panic attack. Her money supply lay dead on the floor. Uan and Manow explained to Star that her husband had supported her with drug money—a light bulb went on. They showed her the drugs. They explained how some gang members had followed her husband into the apartment. They told her she needed to leave Chiang Mai. Her husband's dealings put her in grave danger. If she wanted to live, she would need to return to Buriram permanently. Star felt angry.

As Uan and Manow worked the crime scene, they gave Star time to grab whatever she could carry. She needed to leave immediately. In the widow's state of shock, she never asked the officers what happened to Doc. She wanted to save her own skin. She never thought about others. She never really cared about the American.

In her salvage efforts, the bronze Thai goddess grabbed things quickly. While Pan's team watched, Star took the money out of her strangled husband's wallet. To her, money is the most important thing in life. Without money, she had no self-esteem. She couldn't maintain her beauty. She would have fewer admirers. With John dead on the floor, she considered herself single again.

Star planned to leave Chiang Mai forever. After this gruesome scene, she never wanted to go back to the big city. The ambitious girl felt confident that she could attract another rich man in Buriram. Her new catch would take over her bills, and pay to open a beauty salon there. She would be okay. Although her shallow world collapsed easily, it was just as easily rebuilt.

CHAPTER 43

TOM WALKED UP Huay Kaew Road and stopped at Dunkin' Donuts. He wanted something American. There was no line. From the cute female Thai server, he ordered a chocolate-frosted donut and an orange juice. While waiting in the empty franchise, Tom called to update Daniels. Everything proceeded according to plan.

Daniels congratulated Tom and his team on a job well done. Dr. Jones would be delighted to receive the good news. The operation stopped an important data leak. Ryan talked about the arrival of the PLA's female agent, Ah Kum, in Chiang Mai. Tom needed to devise a plan to eliminate her. Daniels would be in touch with additional intelligence, as the information became available.

Tom decided not to ask Daniels anything about Star. He would try to figure out that piece of the puzzle himself. The two hung up after exchanging a couple hooyahs. With the mission accomplished,

Ryan decided that he would swing by Lucky Massage to celebrate the team's victory. He needed to relieve some stress.

Tom finished his snack and crossed Huay Kaew Road. Just before 7-11, he turned onto the soi where he first met the stunningly gorgeous bronze Thai goddess. The stroll through this area would bring the heartbroken green-faced man closure. He'd been wrong about a number of things. His fantasy ended. He needed to accept reality.

When Tom passed Cat's area, he saw a beautiful young Thai lady standing there. Tom recognized Cat's daughter from her photos. Ket recognized the handsome, muscular American from her mother's description.

"Sa waa dii krap."

"Sa waa dii ka."

"Ket?"

"Ka. Doc?"

"Krap."

"Where's your Mom? Where's Cat? I was just stopping by to say 'hi.' "

Tom planned to relay the tragic story of Star to Cat, at least parts of it. For therapy, he needed a trusted listener.

"She passed away."

"Oh, no. I'm sorry. We were good friends."

"Yeah, she told me about you. She wanted us to meet."

"What happened? I saw her a few days ago. She seemed fine—happy and healthy."

"She'd been suffering from cancer. Mom didn't want anyone to know. Didn't want to trouble anyone. She died peacefully."

"I'm incredibly sorry. She was a good woman. A good friend."

"And a great mother too."

"I'm sure she was. I could tell how much she loved you, Ket. She looked out for you."

Ket became teary eyed. Tom paused. His Thai wife story would need to wait.

"Are you going to be working here from now on?"

"At least for a while, until I wrap up my Mom's affairs."

"I'll come by again soon."

Tom shook his head.

"If there's anything I can do, let me know."

"Thanks. That's very kind. Nice to meet you finally."

"You too. Sorry it was under these circumstances. I wish your Mom were here to introduce us. I'll see you again, Ket."

"I'd like that. I'd ... I'd like that a lot."

Ket wiped her eyes.

"Good-bye for now. Please take care, Ket."

"Good-bye ka."

Tom continued. Cat's passing upset him. He needed to suppress his urge to communicate about

Star. Tom missed a call from Pan. Her text indicated the remainder of the op was proceeding according to plan. Uan and Manow were busy filling out reports, and using their contacts in the police to get the bodies removed. Star was on her way back to Buriram. She was already in Lamphun.

Pan added that she wanted to model the stolen wardrobe items for him. She mentioned a catsuit. Although Tom wasn't ready for it yet, he would be soon enough. He messaged that the team had done a wonderful job and that they would get together soon. He wished them well with the rest of the cleanup.

Once home, Tom showered. He fixed a strong drink and thought about Cat. She helped him meet Star initially. Cat translated. Surely, Cat and Ket weren't connected to Daniels. Surely, Cat was Ket's real mother. Surely, Cat died of cancer, as Ket had told him. When Tom last met Cat, she'd appeared remarkably healthy. He scratched his head.

Cat was a nice lady. Tom never suspected cancer. She died young. As her proud mother claimed, Ket is a lovely and well-educated woman. Her English is perfect. Tom owed it to Cat to keep a watchful eye on Ket. His thoughts drifted to Star. Tom's mood was unfamiliar. He tried hard to let his dream Thai wife go. A tear ran down his cheek. His emotions wandered down empty streets in his mind.

Depressing thoughts of Joy washed over Tom, as he became nostalgic. His little Lolita's suicide troubled him more than ever. He lost many friends before, but they were all SEAL brothers. While serving their country, they perished in battle. They died for a cause. Joy hung herself in a massage parlor and was raped by a necrophiliac. The green-faced man blamed himself for her death, and the death of their unborn child.

Thoughts of Joy convinced Tom that the right Thai woman is still out there waiting to be discovered. Joy and he had gotten along so well. These setbacks wouldn't stop Tom in his quest for a Thai wife. With the alcohol induced burst of energy and a renewed optimism, he decided to go out for a massage.

Chapter 44

WHILE TOM WAITED for his tuk-tuk, he finished another Maker's Mark. The driver suggested he go to Best Body Massage off Canal Road. Tom agreed. Less than ten minutes later, he rewarded his driver with a generous tip. The man drove away smiling. Tom planned to walk back.

As the handsome American arrived at the entrance, a lovely Thai girl looked up from her mobile. She was alone. She greeted the muscular man at the door.

"You need massage with me, MISter?"

"Yes, I do. I do."

"Oil good ka."

"Yes, oil massage. Two hours."

"Two hour, seven-hundred baht. You okay ka?"

"Yes. Yes, that's fine."

"Shoe there. Take seat here. Wash feet first ka."

"Okay."

Tom placed his shoes next to a pair of sexy heels and sat down. The petite masseuse returned with a tub of lukewarm water, in which floated a few fresh-lemon halves. With great enthusiasm, she began washing his feet.

"You name ka?"

"I'm Doc."

"You doctor?"

"Yes, I'm a doctor."

"Big man ka. Rich man."

"Déjà vu."

"Arai ka?"

"Nothing. That's good."

"Ka."

They smiled. Tom shook his head. Issarn girls, scattered all over the country, spoke the same vernacular and possessed the same mannerisms. They thought the same way about farangs. Chiang Mai twisted Tom's moral code, just as her big-brother, Bangkok, had done earlier. He wondered where things were heading. He had a pretty good idea.

"What's your name?"

"Me Nok ka. Nok mean 'bird.' "

"Nice to meet you, Nok."

"Ka."

Employing the fresh lemons, Nok scrubbed Tom's feet. Her actions tickled, and he shifted his legs. When he caught her staring at the bulge in his shorts, she giggled. She wondered about his size, shape, and color. Few men who visited the shop were as handsome as he was.

Nok placed a worn towel in her lap. She dried Tom's feet and handed him a pair of slippers. She led him into a massage room. Nok asked him to remove his clothes. She would return. Tom stripped and lay down.

"Ready ka?"

"Yes, come in."

"Ka."

Nok prepped Tom and stimulated him wildly, as he lay on his stomach. Her technique reminded him of Joy. While using a great deal of fragrant coconut oil, Nok worked his back and legs. She commented on his frog tattoo. Utilizing her body weight, she pumped up and down on his buttocks, where she focused her attention.

Occasionally, Nok touched Tom's testicles. She couldn't put her finger on it, but she felt something odd. Her curiosity got the best of her, and she turned him over. His massive size stunned her. Her probing revealed that he had three balls. Nok's previous customers only possessed two.

Nok guessed a man his size required three balls, and didn't ask any questions. She didn't want to appear ignorant and lose face. She continued her exploration freely. Tom decided not to explain his polyorchidism. She seemed comfortable. He enjoyed her touch.

Nok offered Tom a special massage for 500 baht, and he happily accepted. After what he'd done and been through, he needed a release. When she felt herself getting aroused, she offered to remove her clothes. He agreed to pay the pretty-faced girl an additional 500 baht for fellatio, if she swallowed. She agreed.

When Tom climaxed in Nok's mouth, he forced her head down and thought of ladyboy Bpee. His Thai bird swallowed many times, to avoid drowning. She never experienced any one that deep in her throat, or such a huge volume of semen. A cha-grinned Nok gasped, and her face turned a bright red.

"MISter, you come too much. You three ball ka. Me swallow your baby."

Tom smiled.

"What you name, MISter?"

"I told you. I'm Doc."

"You giant size, MISter."

"That felt good, Nok. Thank you."

"Kem mahk ka."

"Thanks."

"Yin dee ka."

After releasing his sexual tension, Tom relaxed. Nok finished the massage. She drank some water. He showered, dried off vigorously, and got dressed. He paid her, as promised. She was happy with the 1,000-baht bonus. She smiled. Nok licked her lips. Tom smiled. She squeezed his hand affectionately.

"You came back see me ka. Anytime ka. You okay?"

"Sure, Nok. Nice to meet you. I'd like to come again."

Tom smiled.

"Come again soon. Bye ka."

"Good-bye."

"Ka."

While walking back, the Navy SEAL decided he would invite Bpee to Chiang Mai. He fantasized about her often. He felt ready to cross that forbidden line. For the moment though, Tom thought about how wonderful Thai women are and about continuing his search for a Thai wife. His Thai wife was out there somewhere, just waiting to be discovered.

***

Although the coronavirus claimed my parents, I thanked it for confining me. COVID-19 brought me Cam-Tu and Bim, and gave me the opportunity to put my Nobel touch on The Thai Wife Story Star. *While the contagion spreads, it delays my rendezvous with Ying Yue Jiang. I'll transition into* The Thai Wife Story Sugar.

I'm glad Tom survived Star. I hope he'll settle down with the right girl in Sugar. My curiosity about Pan remains. I would like to see him get involved with the PhD student Mim. She's well educated. Or, Ket. I don't want to see him getting mixed up with ladyboys. He wants to meet Bpee. My own limitations are getting in Tom's way.

I double-click the Sugar folder. I open Part1 Sugar. While WORD does its thing, I walk to the edge of the room with my glass of Maker's Mark. I think about Cam-Tu and Bim. I think about Ying Yue and Ae-Cha Lee. I think about the terrible situation in our country. I'm glad I un-locked the novels. I hope the lockdown ends soon. I need to get out.

I stare at the Naval Academy's Chapel.

THAI TO ENGLISH DICTIONARY

A

angrit *English*
aow *to want*
arai *what*
aroy *delicious*

B

baan *house*
boom-boom *slang for sexual intercourse*
bpak *mouth*
bplah meuk *octopus*

C

cha nom yen *Thai milk tea*
cha yen *ice tea*
chah *slow*
chah chah *slowly*
cheu *name*
chi *to use*
chok dee *good luck*
chooay dooay *help*
chorp *like*

D

daeng *red*
dai *can*
dee *good*
dee gwah *good or better*
di chan *polite way of saying 'me' (female)*
doi *mountain*
dooay *also*

G

gai *chicken*
gai yaang khao neeaw *grilled chicken with sticky rice*
geek *a girlfriend who receives large amounts of financial support, usually in return for sexual favors*
gern *a lot*
glang *middle*
gow *nine*

H

haa *five*
haa sip *fifteen*
huay *stream*

J

jing-jing *really*
joop *kiss*
joop, joop *kisses*

K

ka *polite female ending word*
kaew *glass*

kem *salty*

khao ka moo *pork with rice*

khao neeaw ma muang *yellow mango with sticky rice*

khun *you, sir*

khwam suk *happiness or feeling of happiness*

kitteung *miss*

koh *island*

koo muang *moat*

korp khun *thank you*

kor-toht *excuse me*

kow jai *understand*

kow jai mai *do you understand*

kow dtom *rice soup*

krang *times, as in an expression such as 'two times'*

krap *polite male ending word*

kwah *right*

kway teaw ladna *stir-fried rice noodles*

L

lor *handsome*

lor mahk *very handsome*

luk *child*

M

mahk *a lot or very*

mai *no*

mai kow jai *don't understand*

manow *lemon*

mee *to have*

mee khwam suk *to be happy or to have happiness*
meu *hand*
moo dat deo *dried pork*

N

naka *a deeper meaning polite-ending word, expressing more than ka*
nam bplow *drinking water*
nam-dtahn *sugar*
natee *minute (referring to time)*
nee *this*
neeaw *sticky*
neung *one*
nid noi *little*
nok *bird*
nong *used to refer to a younger brother*

P

pahsah *language*
pan *thousand*
pang *expensive*
pom *I or sir*
poot *speak*
prick kee noo *Thai chilies*

R

reo *fast*
ruam gan *total*
ruea *boat*

S

sahm *three*
sahm sip *thirty*
sahy *left*
sala *pavilion*
sanuk *fun*
saphan *bridge*
see *four*
see sip *fourteen*
set *to finish or to orgasm*
sip *ten*
som tam *papaya salad*
som-o *pomelo*
sooay *beautiful*
sorng *two*

T

tam mai *why*
tee-rak *sweetheart*
tom yum goong *hot and sour spicy soup with shrimp*
turagit *business*

U

uan *fat*

V

veena *moon*

W

wan *sweet*

Y

yah bah *a mixture of methamphetamine and caffeine*
yai *large*
Yippon *Japan*
yut *stop*

THE THAI WIFE
SERIES OF NOVELS

THE MAIN NARRATOR is a Nobel laureate in literature, awarded for his writings about Thailand. He discovers unfinished novels in his apartment in Annapolis, Maryland. As he begins to edit, bringing them to the Nobel level, the coronavirus pandemic strikes. It wreaks havoc on his family. While dealing with personal issues, including numerous affairs, the Nobel laureate relays the story of Doctor Adventure.

Doc is a decorated Navy SEAL and cybersecurity expert. His polyorchidism results in an unusually high testosterone level. His intensity leads to questionable behavior in the field, and Doc is fired from the National Security Agency. He continues covert operations in Thailand, as a critical but underground asset. He conducts cyber operations against the Chinese. His cover involves exploring Thailand's massage parlors and bars.

Doc falls in love with a series of gorgeous Thai ladies. Each time that he is about to pop the big question, disaster strikes. He continues his quest for finding the perfect Thai wife through dozens of intense encounters. He meets several ladyboys, and his own sexuality is called into question.

Completed in the Thai Wife Series of Novels

The Thai Wife Story Joy (Book 1)

The Thai Wife Story Star (Book 2)

Planned

The Thai Wife Story Sugar (Book 3)

The Thai Wife Story Gun (Book 4)

The Thai Wife Story Patty (Book 5)

The Thai Wife Story Opal (Book 6)

The Thai Wife Story Apple (Book 7)

The Thai Wife Story Peach (Book 8)

The Thai Wife Story Moon (Book 9)

The Thai Wife Story Ying (Book 10)

THE THAI WIFE STORY
SUGAR: PREVIEW

THE FOLLOWING IS a preview of the first chapter of the novel *The Thai Wife Story Sugar*. The actual version of chapter one may differ.

CHAPTER 1
(Preview of *The Thai Wife Story Sugar*)

I STOP STARING AT the Naval Academy's Chapel. I sit down. I open the file Part1 Sugar. I'm glad the Navy SEAL, Tom, is doing well. He's intent on finding a Thai wife. It's too bad he couldn't marry Joy or Star. He thinks Joy committed suicide. The ladyboy Bpee lied to him. I'm glad he's steering clear of ladyboys. Star was married already. Thanks to the green-faced man, she's a widow. I hope Sugar is the right Thai girl. I continue with my Nobel level of editing.

Tom dropped by unannounced to see Pan at the My Tee-Rak Bar on Loi Kroh Road in downtown Chiang Mai. As the Navy SEAL approached the bar, he recognized Pan's gorgeous, tan Thai legs. She wore a red crop top, black miniskirt, and red stilettos, which formerly belonged to Star. Pan stood out from the rest of the Thai bargirls, not only at the My Tee-Rak Bar, but among all those whom he'd walked past on Loi Kroh.

The Navy SEAL heard German being spoken. Two blond-haired men solicited Pan. Tom remained at a distance. One German rested a hand on her lovely shoulder. The other kissed the Si Saket girl on her lips. From Tom's vantage point, she returned the man's kiss. Disappointed, the green-faced man retraced his steps. Pan missed him. His head drooped.

What do you expect? Pan works in a bar. She needs money. When a customer buys her a lady drink, she gets a percentage. She's a nice girl. Don't give up. She's not going to sleep with those guys.

Tom was right to walk away. I wouldn't want him fighting the Germans. If he injured them that might cause problems with Dr. Jones and the agency. Tom needs to remain below the radar. He has an important mission to conduct. Maker's Mark does my talking. Tom is sober. Don't listen to me, ole boy.

Tom walked in the direction of the Koo Muang—the moat surrounding the ancient city of Chiang Mai.

"Hey, handsome man. You need massage ka?"

"You good shape, MISter."

"No thanks. I'm okay."

Pretty girl 1 → "Handsome man."

Pretty girl 2 → "Massage ka?"

"Not tonight."

"When ka?"

Tom shook his head.

"Me li-eh you ka."

With each massage parlor Tom passed, pretty Thai girls offered him their services. Some girls touched him.

"MISter, you need special massage ka?"

"Oil good, MISter."

"No expensive."

Drunk Thai bargirl → "Me wery good girl."

Pretty ladyboy → "Where you go?"

Sexy Thai girl → "One hour, MISter?"

"Massage ka?"

"Come here, MISter."

"Thanks. I'm okay."

Feminine ladyboy → "Special?"

Small ladyboy → "I know you ka."

"No, you don't."

Tom checked out the ladyboys, as he walked past the Friends Corner Bar. Several looked up from their mobiles.

The masseuses, bargirls, and ladyboys were in their late 20s and early 30s. They applied heavy makeup, to restore their lost youths. In the dimly lit soi, they looked good. Tom came for Pan though. None of the others interested him. If he was going to try a ladyboy, Bpee would be first.

Steer clear of ladyboys, ole boy.

"Where you go?" A tuk-tuk driver asked.

Tom didn't respond. He drifted.

Sexy girl 1 → "Massage ka?"

Sexy girl 2 → "You need full body, MISter?"

"You want special? Mai pang."

The massage girls lined both sides of the narrow street. Tom continued, and ignored their offers. He passed a mamasan. Her two white dogs sat out front on a table, and wagged their tails. One of the girls whom the mamasan offered appeared to be her daughter. Like the boat man at the Saphan Taksin Pier in Bangkok, the most persistent and loudest workers got the majority of customers. As the night wore on, and farangs became intoxicated, the girls became more beautiful. The night owls earned the biggest tips.

When the Navy SEAL reached the end of Loi Kroh Road, he turned right on Kotchasarn Road. Tom passed the Lucky Bar. It stayed open until 9:00 AM, despite the law requiring all bars to close by 1:30 AM. The odor from the Koo Muang bothered him. Its stagnant water added to the humidity. Chiang Mai gave him a wet slap across the face. He kept going.

The Navy SEAL longed for American food. He walked past Chiang Mai Elephant Land, Chai Massage, ladyboys, POP Big Bike Rental, Aroon Rai Restaurant, free lancers, Bo Hanuman Tattoo Cave, backpackers, an ATM, Shaman Bookshop, Busstop BBQ, Maomunkung Seafood, Sorn Chan Restaurant, Dang Bike Hire, Imm Hotel Tapae, Smile

Food & Beverage, Lek's Fish Foot Spa, and Klang Ya Tapae Pharmacy. Across from Tapae Gate, there were five tuk-tuks parked in front of McDonald's. When Tom smelled the food, his mouth began watering.

Tuk-tuk driver 1 → "Where you go, MISter?"

Tuk-tuk driver 2 → "Me have lady."

Chiang Mai got the best of the American. He'd seen a lot on his walk. Tom put his desire for a burger and fries on hold, and followed his desire for a Thai lady. The McDonald's was open 24-7.

During the COVID-19 pandemic, the McDonald's is only open until 9:00 PM. It even shut down completely for a while. The Lucky Bar is closed, as is Lek's Fish Foot Spa. Aroon Rai, which had been in business for over 60 years, even closed. The lockdown has killed tourism in Thailand. I worry about the Thai people. Many have lost their jobs. The country relies too heavily on tourism. Bangkok is a real bottleneck. It's classified as a dark-red zone.

When the coronavirus spreads through the factories in Bangkok, I hope they don't send workers back to their villages. That would be a terrible super-spreader event. I hope they've ordered plenty of vaccines from multiple sources. I wouldn't want them to put all their eggs in one basket. That could spell disaster for the wonderful Thai people, especially the kind people of Issarn. They know very little about modern medicine.

"Sayuri krap."

"MISter, girls wery expensive Sayuri. Me know good place krap."

"Forget it."

Tom moved to the next tuk-tuk driver.

"Wait, MISter."

"You missed your chance."

"MISter?"

Tom asked the next tuk-tuk driver, "How much to go to Sayuri?"

"Oh, Sayuri. It wery far, MISter."

"I know where it is. Tow rai?"

"For you, cheap price, only one-hundred and fifty baht."

"I can give you eighty."

"MISter, Sayuri wery far."

Tom moved to the next tuk-tuk driver.

"I'll give you eighty baht to take me to Sayuri."

"Ka pom."

The disappointed tuk-tuk drivers glared at the driver who was trying to make an honest living. After their histrionics, they went back to their mobiles. They hoped for a gullible tourist.

The tuk-tuk retraced the Navy SEAL's walk, and sped along the Koo Muang, past the Easy Corner Bar, down Loi Kroh, past White Orchid Massage, past Young & Beautiful Massage, past Super Rich Chiang Mai, and past Pan's bar. Tom didn't spot her or the Germans. He wondered about Pan. The tuk-tuk continued on a narrow soi to the bank of the Ping River, crossed Saphan Nawarat, and merged onto Charoen Muang Road, until turning left onto Bumruang Rajd Road. The breeze generated cooled Tom. The noise prevented rational thought. The tuk-tuk slowed and turned. Tom saw the Sayuri Massage Parlor and Entertainment Complex.

"Sayuri krap."

Tom gave the driver 100 baht.

"Keep it."

"Korp khun krap."

"I'll be a while. No need to wait."

"Ka pom. I here krap."

"Suit yourself."

"Krap."

When the Navy SEAL entered the massage complex, a blast of cold air and a smell of eucalyptus greeted him. A small Thai man led him to a sofa in front of a large window. Behind it, sat dozens of scantily clad young Thai girls, wearing numbers. Through the fish bowl, they began flirting with Tom, and with their tiny hands, waved and blew kisses. They were all pretty. They were all in high heels.

"Drink?"

"Yeah, diet coke."

"We regular coke. No have coke zero."

"Okay. Regular coke."

"Krap."

'Sayuri' is a Japanese word meaning 'small lily.' The soapy massage parlor's patrons were older Japanese men. They came to make their dreams about small flower girls a reality. The men focused their eyes on the lilies. Out of respect, they didn't look at their compatriots. The Navy SEAL scanned the gallery with his sniper eyes.

"Here, sir. One-hundred and fifty baht krap."

"Thanks."

Tom handed the Myanmar waiter two 100-baht bills.

"Keep it."

"Thank."

Although none of the girls were as attractive as Pan, Tom narrowed his choice down to a pair of lookers. A Japanese man took Tom's first choice. Being scooped prompted him into action. He called over the man distributing the girls.

"How old is number sip gow?"

"She eighteen. Wirgin."

Tom restrained his laughter. He smiled.

"Tow rai krap?"

"Two-thousand, five-hundred baht. Wirgin expensive krap."

"I'll take her. Not a virgin much longer."

The man didn't understand.

"Ka pom."

While the man signaled for number 19 to come out, Tom drank his coke. He stood up. The man led him to a cashier. Tom paid.

"Some tip for me ka?" the cashier asked.

Tom gave the girl 20 baht. She smiled. He gave the man signaling the girls 50 baht. He smiled.

Number 19 arrived. She gripped Tom's hand affectionately. They walked, and exchanged smiles.

"Ha-low. You handsome man. What name you?"

"I'm Doc."

"You doctor?"

"Yes," Tom lied.

"Wow! You big man. Rich man ka."

"What's your name?"

"Me Pim."

"Pim?"

"Ka. Pim."

"Nice to meet you, Pim."

"Nice meet you, Doc. He, he, he."

Pim led Tom through a dimly lit corridor. They passed a cleaning lady. Pim took him down uneven stairs to their room.

"You first time Sayuri?"

"Yeah, been looking forward to coming here."

Pim missed his meaning. She opened the creaky door. Tom entered. The masseuse locked the door. He saw an inflatable mattress on the floor, a bed with white sheets, a shower, towels, and a laundry basket—containing soap, shampoo, mouthwash, condoms, and other sundry articles. Pim smiled naughtily.

"Remove clothes ka. Take shower first. He, he, he."

BOOKS BY
RAYMOND GREENLAW

The Thai Wife Story Joy (also available in electronic form), Book 1 of *The Thai Wife Series of Novels.*

The Thai Wife Story Star (also available in electronic form), Book 2 of *The Thai Wife Series of Novels.*

Palmarès (also available in electronic form).

Raymond's Checklist for Traveling in the USA (also available in electronic form), Book 1 of *Raymond's Checklist Series.*

Raymond's Checklist for Traveling in Thailand (also available in electronic form), Book 2 of *Raymond's Checklist Series.*

Raymond's Checklist for Traveling the World (also available in electronic form), Book 3 of *Raymond's Checklist Series.*

Raymond's Checklist for His Personal Bucket List (also available in electronic form), Book 4 of *Raymond's Checklist Series.*

Raymond's Checklist for Gear for a Long Hike (also available in electronic form), Book 5 of *Raymond's Checklist Series.*

Raymond's Checklist Cycling Gear (also available in paperback form), Book 6 of *Raymond's Checklist Series.*

The Hazards of Cycling in Thailand: Guidelines for Tourists (also available in electronic form).

Trapped in Thailand's Cave (also available in electronic form).

The Pacific Crest Trail: Its Fastest Hike, second edition (also available in electronic form).

Bob: My Dad, the Fisherman: A Father and Son's Relationship (also available in electronic form).

(with Saowaluk Rattanaudomsawat) *Essential Conversational Thai: Learn to Speak Thai Quickly, while Traveling in Thailand.*

You'll Never Walk Alone: Love Poems for My Sweetheart (also available in electronic form).

Poems of Raymond Greenlaw, 1986–2005 (also available in electronic form).

The Fastest Hike across Thailand (expected October 2021).

About the Author

RAYMOND "WALL" Greenlaw was born in Providence, Rhode Island, USA to Roxy and Bob. Raymond has always enjoyed nature, big trees, lakes, mountains, and the sea. He writes about a wide range of topics and is the author of more than 35 books.